Safe Harbor

Elizabeth Penney

AnniesFiction.com

Books in the Inn at Magnolia Harbor series

Where Hope Blooms
Safe Harbor
Binding Vows

. . . and more to come!

Library of Congress-in-Publication Data
Safe Harbor / by Elizabeth Penney
p. cm.
I. Title
                    2018962794

AnniesFiction.com
(800) 282-6643
The Inn at Magnolia Harbor™
Series Creator: Shari Lohner
Editor: Jane Haertel
Cover Illustrator: Bonnie Leick

10 11 12 13 14 | Printed in China | 9 8 7 6 5 4 3 2

Grace

"What a beautiful day. And it's supposed to be a perfect week." Grace Porter stepped out onto the inn's wraparound porch and paused to appreciate the gorgeous May morning. Bushes, trees, and flower beds were in bloom, releasing enticing scents into the soft, warm air. Birds chirped and sang, and squirrels performed a comical dance dashing up and down tree trunks.

"Glad to hear it." Charlotte Wylde's voice was slightly muffled behind the pile of red-and-white bunting she held. "That means a lot of visitors for Strawberry Fest." Although other South Carolina towns celebrated the delectable fruit, this was the first year for Magnolia Harbor. The members of the small chamber of commerce had their fingers crossed it would be a success.

Grace set up a stepladder and positioned it near the front door. "We're noticing a difference already. As of today we're fully booked, and that wasn't true this week last year." Grace and Charlotte, her younger sister, had owned the Magnolia Harbor Inn for the past seven years. Their combination of skills worked well together, forming a harmonious partnership that had renovated the 1816 mansion into a showplace.

Charlotte dropped the bunting onto the polished floorboards. "Am I climbing the ladder or are you?" She rested her hands on her hips and regarded the tall facade. The inn had three stories, including a veranda on the second floor. "I know you don't like ladders."

Grace didn't, but she could handle a stepladder with no problem.

"I'll do it." She pulled a staple gun out of her apron pocket. "You can hand me the fabric as I go." She climbed as high as she could, noticing that it would still require a stretch of her arms to reach the top of the door.

"Don't get on the top step," Charlotte warned. "It's not safe."

Grace smiled at her sister's concern. "I won't." She waved a hand in a come-on gesture. "Ready when you are."

Charlotte fed her the fabric, which Grace twisted and stapled above the door. "I'm thinking of entering the chef's contest," Charlotte said. The festival was featuring a cook-off of strawberry main dishes from chefs in the area. The entries would be featured at the dinner dance held on the last night.

"You should," Grace said. "You're a shoo-in." Charlotte was not only an experienced chef, she was the author of several best-selling cookbooks and counting. The inn only served breakfast and evening hors d'oeuvres, so she rarely got an opportunity to put her entrée-making skills on display.

"Maybe I will." Charlotte handed Grace another length of cloth. "Dean's going to enter." Dean Bradley owned The Tidewater, an inn and restaurant across Lake Haven. After a rocky past working relationship, he and Charlotte were now friends.

"Sounds like fun, then." Grace winked at her sister. "Maybe you can beat him."

Charlotte scoffed. "No maybe about it."

Grace knew that prodding Charlotte's competitive side was a sure way to get her creative juices flowing. Her sister was never happier than when dreaming up new culinary delights. Even better, Grace and anyone else in the vicinity would get to sample a new Charlotte Wylde creation.

The phone rang inside. "I knew I should have grabbed the handheld," Grace said.

"I'll get it. Hang on." Charlotte hurried through the screen door, her blonde hair flying. As she went in, Winston trotted out. The inn's resident dog, a shih tzu mix, trotted over to check on Grace, then laid on the top veranda step and emitted a sigh.

"Hey, Winston. Come to keep an eye on us?" Grace set the stapler down and leaned on the ladder, not bothering to get down. It really was a lovely day. If she got everything done, maybe she'd take a sunset kayak ride on the lake. A peaceful paddle was the perfect way to relax.

A minivan pulled into the driveway and, as the vehicle drew closer, Grace spotted a woman driving and the heads of three children in the back. They were expecting a couple more guests today—a woman and a couple—and this didn't look like them. The van rolled to a stop and the doors flew open. The passengers climbed out.

To her amusement, she saw that the group was wearing strawberry costumes consisting of baggy suits, red tights, and green caps that resembled stems. *What is this all about?*

Winston perked up at the sight of visitors and rose to his feet, tail wagging. Then one of the children broke away and darted across the lawn, right toward the fountain. "Sam, stop!" his mother shouted, but the boy kept on going. Barking, Winston raced toward the boy. He adored children and no doubt wanted to help.

Grace took a step down but missed the rung and stumbled. *Oh, no.* Her arms windmilled as she struggled to remain upright.

Then a firm hand caught her under the elbow. "Don't worry, I'm a doctor," a low voice said, the man's tone holding a hint of laughter.

Grace looked down to see Dr. Curt King, one of the guests. "I'm glad you were there." She steadied herself and checked on the boy. He was almost to the fountain, his hapless mother trying to catch up. Fortunately the other two children were waiting by the path.

"I was around the corner," Curt said. He took in the situation and burst into action, racing across the lawn at an angle and grabbing Sam, who was teetering on the edge of the basin. Winston danced around, barking, then settled once the boy was safe.

His mother joined Curt and the child, a hand to her chest as she panted. "Thank you so much." She hunkered down beside Sam. "What did I tell you about listening to Mommy?"

The child thrust out his bottom lip. "That I have to?"

All the adults burst into laughter, including Charlotte, who had slipped back outside. "I guess I missed the excitement," Charlotte said.

In company with Curt and Winston, the woman and her brood strolled up the path. "Too bad my husband had to go in to the hospital to work," the woman said. "I could have used his help."

"Oh, does he practice at Northshore Medical Center?" Curt's tone was light but Grace sensed something more than casual interest.

"Yes, he does. Dr. Paul Greenlaw. He's a general practitioner and had to check on some patients who had surgery." The woman smiled. "He's good that way."

Curt cleared his throat. "An old . . . friend of mine works there. Presley Baker."

Charlotte elbowed Grace, who smiled. By the blush on the young doctor's face, Grace guessed the young woman was more than a friend. Or had been, anyway.

"Presley? Oh, she's wonderful." The woman reached the bottom of the steps. "Good morning. I'm Laura Greenlaw and we're here for the strawberry costume contest." She pointed to each child, two boys and a girl. "We're The Wild Strawberries."

Grace could see the logic of that name. Wild strawberries were tiny—and sweet. And in this case, rather unruly. One of them, anyway. After making introductions, Grace said, "I'm sorry. It's great to meet you and see these adorable costumes, but there isn't a contest here."

Laura foraged in a pocket hidden somewhere in the depths of her costume. She pulled out a rectangle of newsprint. "But this advertisement lists the inn as a judging station."

Grace took the piece of paper, seeing that it was the full-page ad the chamber had put in about the festival. Sure enough, under the costume contest was a list of businesses participating. Magnolia Harbor Inn was one of them.

"I'm sorry." Grace shook her head in regret. "But they made a mistake. You'll have to go to one of the other places."

"But your costumes are adorable." Charlotte gave them a thumbs-up. "Good luck."

Laura wrinkled her nose as she studied the ad. "All right, we'll do that. Come on kids." On the path she paused to call, "Nice to meet you." The others chorused agreement.

"I wonder how many more costumed visitors we're going to get," Charlotte said after Laura herded her children into the van and drove away.

Grace checked the date of the paper and groaned softly. "A ton, I bet. The paper only comes out weekly so it's too late for a correction."

Charlotte folded her arms, tapping one foot as she thought. "That's true. But maybe they can fix it on their website and on social media. I'll call and see."

"After we do the bunting, okay?" Grace asked. "I hate to leave it half done."

"Want a hand?" Curt asked. "I'm not doing anything right now."

The women accepted his help, resulting in the rest of the decorations going up in record time. Winston supervised from his favorite position on the steps.

"Time for sweet tea," Charlotte said when they'd finished. "Shall I bring out a pitcher?"

Grace settled into one of the wicker armchairs with a sigh. "That sounds wonderful. Want to join us, Curt?"

"I'd love a glass of tea. Need any help?" he asked Charlotte, revealing he was a gentleman as well as a doctor.

"I'm all set, thanks," Charlotte said. "I'll bring a plate of lemon cookies too. My new recipe." The screen door closed behind Charlotte.

"Your sister is a great cook," Curt said. He patted his midriff. "I haven't eaten a breakfast like that in years." In honor of the festival, Charlotte had whipped up some baked strawberry pancakes, served with local bacon and sausage on the side. Real maple syrup they ordered from Vermont was a signature touch.

"We have signed copies of her cookbooks for sale." Grace laughed to show him she was joking. No high-pressure tactics here.

"Maybe I'll buy one for my mom." Curt was silent for a moment. "Actually, I should purchase one for myself. I get tired of cafeteria food, even though our hospital's meals aren't bad." Grace knew from his registration that he lived in Greenville, South Carolina.

"They're pretty good at our hospital too. I've eaten there while visiting friends."

"Do you know Presley Baker?" he asked. "She's an obstetrics nurse there."

The intensity in his voice made Grace turn to look at him. His hazel eyes were somber. "I don't. But maybe she's new to town." Winston, who was sensitive to guest moods, trotted over to lie beside his chair.

He rubbed a hand down his pant leg. "She just moved to Magnolia Harbor. We went to college together at Duke University."

"That's a fine school." As she heard each new bit of information, Grace's sense that there was a story here grew.

The screen door opened and Charlotte burst through carrying a tray. She set it on a low table after moving a vase of flowers aside.

"You're not joining us?" Grace asked. There were only two glasses on the tray.

When everything was arranged to her satisfaction, Charlotte straightened. "No, I'm going to get working on recipes. Figure out a sure winner." She grinned. "And before you ask, I already called the paper. They're going to post a correction online."

"Go, Charlotte." Grace poured a glass of tea for Curt. "By the way, who called us earlier?"

"Someone booking for next week." Charlotte strode across the porch. "Enjoy."

After serving tea, Grace passed the plate of cookies to her guest. "So you and Presley went to college together. I have a lot of good friends from my Clemson days."

Curt sipped his tea and selected a lemon-frosted sugar cookie. Then he said, "She was my first girlfriend. We got engaged and then"—he sighed—"I blew it."

Grace remained silent, letting him lead the conversation. One of the unexpected aspects of owning an inn was how often she became a confidante for guests. While many were in Magnolia Harbor only on a pleasure trip, others were seeking something more. If she could offer a listening ear, some encouragement, even advice at times, well, that was very rewarding.

Others had done the same for her at critical points.

"Yeah," Curt went on. "I was kind of full of myself back then." He tapped his chest. "I was going to be a doctor and set the world on fire. There wasn't room for my ego *and* Presley in our relationship. So she broke it off when we were seniors."

"And you've had regrets." Grace's voice was soft.

"That's right." He sighed again. "Regrets. So I'm here to tell her that." He gave a rueful laugh. "If I dare. It's one thing in theory, but now that I'm here . . ." His voice trailed off.

He had cold feet. And that was understandable. "Well, what's the worst thing that can happen?" Grace asked.

Another rueful laugh. "She might not want to talk to me."

Grace winced. "That would sting." She paused, then said, "But at least you would know you gave your love another chance. Right now she has no idea how you feel about her. And vice versa."

Curt took another cookie and crunched, appearing to consider her words.

She didn't press the subject further, sensing she'd given him plenty to think about. Now it was up to this place to do the rest. The Magnolia Harbor Inn worked a special kind of magic on all who sheltered in it, whether they were seeking wisdom, healing, or help. Grace had no doubt the young doctor's life would be transformed. Exactly how was still a mystery.

Anne

The deeper they drove into South Carolina, the bigger the knot in Anne Montgomery's belly grew. For the past three hours, she and Davis, her husband of thirty-five years, had been sailing down the interstate from Charlotte, North Carolina. They'd left bustling city traffic behind, and on either side rolling countryside sweltered under a humid haze. It was only May but summer had arrived.

"Can't you give me a clue where we're going?" Anne glanced at Davis, who was intent yet relaxed behind the wheel of their brand-new SUV. Although recently retired, he was still trim and tanned, with a full head of gray hair. Handsome. Intelligent. *Perfect.* In general, and for her. Oh, how she loved him.

But they hadn't been alone, truly alone, miles from the office and family, in years. Anne clutched the armrest, stage fright gripping her. She'd forgotten her lines. What if . . .

Davis smiled, eyes flashing behind metal-rimmed specs. "I could, but I won't. Sit back and relax, Anne. This weekend is all about you." He turned his gaze back to the road, signaled to pass a slow-moving truck. "Me. Us."

Us. Anne pondered the notion. Who were they, really? The good-looking couple active in social circles in the growing city of Charlotte, Davis a descendant of a proud first family? The owners of the flourishing accounting practice now helmed by their only son, Austin? A man and woman who had fallen deeply in love thirty-some years ago?

Then the routine demands of marriage and work had slowly pulled them apart. But there'd always been a wedge between them, even in the beginning, and it was her fault.

They reached the intersection with Interstate 95, the traffic snarling again at this crossroads. Davis slowed, moving to the right lane so they could exit. Perhaps he was heading south, to Hilton Head or Savannah. Both were beautiful destinations favored by couples.

That's what Davis had told her yesterday, that they were taking off for a romantic getaway. He wouldn't say where but had told her to pack a swimsuit, shorts, and a pretty dress or two. "Let's celebrate," he said. "My retirement, this next phase of our life together. A second honeymoon."

It wasn't like her husband to be spontaneous. As suited his profession, he was analytical and methodical. A planner.

He'd brought his golf clubs, of course. There was always time for his favorite sport, second honeymoon or not.

The exit for Interstate 95 South flashed by. Davis slowed even more and put on his signal.

The knot in her belly twisted tighter when he took the northbound exit. Gulping in breaths of air, Anne fought down panic, even as she willed herself to keep still. There were lots of wonderful destinations in that direction. Hilton Head. Charleston.

She closed her eyes as they merged into traffic on the new highway, semis and cars crowding the bumpers, fighting for space. But the vistas of South Carolina's Low Country rolled behind her lids anyway. The cypress swamps, live oaks, and rustic farms.

Unexpected grief bloomed, making tears burn in her eyes. She'd missed the Low Country, this distinctive landscape bred into her bones. Memories flooded in, a cascade of loss and pain. *Regret*.

A warm hand touched her forearm. "Are you awake, Anne? We're almost there."

She must have fallen asleep. They were now driving along a secondary road lined with moss-draped oaks. Behind wrought iron fences, elegant historic homes sat nestled in azalea bushes.

Welcome to Magnolia Harbor, a large sign proclaimed.

Cold shock blasted away the rest of her drowsiness.

Davis had brought Anne to her birthplace, her childhood home. But he couldn't know her history here, right? She studied his beaming face. Or did he?

"Surprised?" he asked. When she didn't answer, his smile faltered. "I saw you'd been checking this place out, thought you might want to visit."

Relief swamped her. He didn't know why she'd been looking up the town. *So dumb, Anne, to leave the computer on that page.* She quickly put a hand on his. "It's beautiful, Davis. One of the prettiest towns in the South. And you know how I love stately Southern homes." Anne was an amateur student of architecture. She enjoyed visiting historic sites and neighborhoods and taking photographs, then learning about the stories behind the buildings. Even in the midst of hardship and pain, people tried to create beauty. That was something Anne liked to keep in mind.

As they drove further into town, Anne seeing the place both as it was and how it used to be, hungry now to take it in, they reached the intersection with Lake Haven Road. The glistening lake lay before them, colorful sails and motorboats dotting the blue. Davis turned left, which led them past the waterfront park with its bandstand and green space and docks. On the other side of the road was a row of storefronts. The actual business district, consisting of cobblestoned Main Street and several side streets, lay on the next block over, Anne remembered.

"What's going on, I wonder?" Anne said. Throngs of people were in the park, where booths were being assembled. They had to stop at crosswalks to allow pedestrians to cross.

Davis pointed at a sign strung across the street. "Strawberry Fest." He laughed. "That's another reason I picked Magnolia Harbor. They're your favorite fruit." He was right, an observation that touched her.

"How thoughtful of you," she said. "I can't wait to indulge." As they drove past the festival, she asked, "How much farther to where we're staying?" She wasn't up to date on lodging options in town.

David consulted the GPS unit on the dash. "Another mile or so."

The storefronts and businesses petered out, replaced by houses. These were a mix of styles of older homes, some with more modern additions squeezed in where space allowed.

Living in a lakefront town was a desirable choice for most people. For Anne, it had been a prison. Though at times she wondered if she'd exchanged one jail for another. The one she occupied now was more to her liking, but almost as restrictive. *You created it yourself*, a voice whispered. *And you have the key* . . . Anne pushed aside those nagging thoughts. She was an expert at pushing them away after all these years.

Davis's phone buzzed. He handed it to Anne. "Can you see who that is?" He strictly obeyed the rules against talking while driving. *Cora Montgomery.* "It's your mother." *Of course.* They'd been gone, what? Not even half a day? If her life was a prison, then Miss Cora was the warden.

"I'll call Mama later." He must have seen her grimace. "Just a quick call to tell her we made it, okay? Then I'm all yours."

Had he ever been, fully? Anne suppressed that line of thinking. She had no right, with her history, to criticize. She regarded his handsome profile, noticing with affection the tiny hint of a double chin under his firm jaw. They were quite a pair. Like her grandmother had said, there was a lid for every pot. They might be a dented, battered old pair but they belonged together, right?

So she hoped. She sucked in a deep breath. This weekend was too important to allow her past to rise up and bite her. Then her belly hollowed with trepidation and she shivered. How long could secrets stay buried? For a moment it was as if they were banging on a locked door, demanding to be released—

"Here we are," Davis said, interrupting her thoughts. "The Magnolia Harbor Inn." He turned between stone urns on posts and drove toward a magnificent antebellum mansion with massive pillars adorning the front of the building.

Anne rolled down the window, breathing deep, the fragrance of the flowers that adorned the grounds soothing her. She remembered this place. It used to be a family home, built by one of Magnolia Harbor's founders. She'd played as a child on the lawns rolling down to the lake.

Davis parked near the front and they climbed out. "I'll get the bags later," he said. "Let's check in."

An image flashed into her mind: Anne and a friend—Lisa Clark—wearing pastel puff-sleeved dresses, new pairs of patent leather Mary Janes on their feet. That was a good memory, a reassuring one, and Anne clung to it as she grabbed her purse and followed Davis across the wide veranda to the door. He held it open with a nod and she entered a spacious foyer, her footsteps echoing on the tiled floor. Above, a crystal chandelier shimmered in the sunlight.

"This way." Davis took her arm and guided her to the front desk, placed to one side. He rang the bell.

While they waited, Anne drank in the atmosphere of genteel luxury, noting it hadn't changed much. Delicate wrought iron railings trimmed the winding staircase and second-floor balconies and the woodwork spoke of fine craftsmanship and age. No one did work like that anymore.

An attractive woman with shoulder-length dark hair and blue eyes bustled from an adjacent room. "Good afternoon," she said with a smile. "I'm Grace Porter, your host." She slid behind the desk. "Sorry to keep you waiting."

Davis moved closer to lean on the countertop. "We didn't mind. It gave us a chance to look around a bit. You've got a lovely place here."

"Thanks. We hope you enjoy your stay with us." Grace tapped at the computer. "I'm guessing you're the Montgomerys."

"That's right." Davis gave her his credit card. "Anne and Davis."

Grace processed the card. She gave him two keys. "I've put you in the Dogwood Suite. It has a lake view and private bath with a soaking tub."

Anne sighed. A long bath sounded divine, the perfect thing to help her relax. Maybe staying in Magnolia Harbor would be all right. It was only for a few days. No one was likely to recognize her, after so much time. She'd try to enjoy it.

"Did you hear that, darling? A room with a lake view." Her husband's eyes twinkled. He turned back to Grace. "I might have time to get in a couple rounds of golf. Is there a place you recommend?"

While Grace showed him nearby golf courses on a printed map, Anne's gaze fell on a rack of brochures featuring local attractions. One in particular caught her eye, the Jackson House Museum. Another family home converted to a new use.

"You should check that out," Grace said, interrupting Anne's thoughts. "The family has a very interesting history." She smiled at them both. "If you're ready, I'll take you up."

The Dogwood Suite was every woman's dream. Davis beamed at Anne's involuntary gasp of pleasure, as if he were personally responsible for its serene beauty. Decorated in pale colors, it featured a four-poster king bed, a fireplace, and French doors to a veranda. Anne opened one and slipped out to drink in the spectacular view of Lake Haven.

Resting her hands on the railing, she savored the warm, soft air teasing through her hair.

"What do you think?" Davis asked. He stepped onto the veranda and closed the door.

Anne turned to Davis, her smile so wide her cheeks hurt. As many emotions as being back in her hometown brought up, the smile was genuine enough. Who knew her by-the-book accountant husband could be so romantic? "I love it. Thank you." She threw herself toward him for a kiss. *Go away*, she told the secrets. *The past doesn't matter, not when I have so much in the present.*

But before she reached him, his phone buzzed. He put up a hand. "Hold that thought, Anne. Mama's calling."

3

Bridget

"Taste these for me." A blonde woman thrust a tray under Bridget's nose.

"What am I looking at?" Bridget O'Brien asked, letting go of her suitcase handle. The tray held six tiny plates, each holding a dab of something that smelled really good. It'd been a long day traveling from Boston, her only sustenance airline crackers and peanuts.

The woman set the tray on the reception counter and pointed. "Those three are strawberry basil chicken and the others are strawberry, chickpea, and asparagus couscous."

"Sounds yummy." Bridget's mouth was watering already. She picked up a small fork and dug in, the woman watching anxiously.

"I'm entering a cooking contest at Strawberry Fest," the cook explained. "These are two dishes I invented this morning." She paused, then added, "I'm Charlotte Wylde, one of the innkeepers."

Bridget laughed. "I thought you might be. I've been looking forward to meeting you." While researching the inn, she'd learned that Charlotte was not only the inn's chef, she was also a best-selling cookbook author. Her glance fell on a display of books nearby, Charlotte's pretty face shining from the cover. Bridget would have to buy a signed copy.

Right now she had the honor of sampling a famous chef's creations and providing feedback. Bridget took her time, allowing the mingled flavors to develop on her tongue. She thought for a minute. "You know what? I'd go with the couscous. The strawberry-asparagus pairing is so unusual—not to mention delicious."

Charlotte nodded. "I'll keep it in the running." She gave Bridget an infectious grin. "I've got a ton more ideas."

Bridget laughed. "So do I. Only I write novels, not cookbooks." She tapped her head. "Too many ideas, too little time."

Charlotte's eyes took on a gleam. "You're a writer?" She leaned a little closer. "I love meeting other writers. They're the only ones who understand."

Her comment didn't need an explanation, as Bridget knew all too well the quirks and peculiarities that came with the profession. On the way to the inn, she'd annoyed fellow drivers with her slow speed as she gawked around at the pretty town, which was the perfect model for the new book she was writing. But of course that wasn't the only thing that had brought her here.

An attractive woman with dark hair entered the foyer, a small dog at her heels. "I thought I heard the bell." She looked at Bridget. "Are you all checked in?"

"She's not, Grace," Charlotte said, her face sheepish. "I waylaid her with my samples."

"And they were wonderful," Bridget said. To Grace she said, "I'm Bridget O'Brien. I booked a single."

Grace cast an amused look at the tray. "I'll try those in a minute. But first let's get Bridget settled." She began to tap on the computer keys.

"Nice meeting you, Bridget," Charlotte said. "Let's talk about writing and books soon." She began bustling away, calling over her shoulder, "I'll put these in the dining room. They'll be waiting for you, Grace."

While she processed the registration, Grace introduced herself and her sweet little dog, Winston. "You're in town at a good time. Strawberry Fest is getting underway, and it's sure to be fun."

Bridget signed the form. "I'm looking forward to checking it out. But the main reason I'm here is to do some research." *For my book and about my family.* As she set the pen down, her hand went to the locket she always wore, a legacy from her birth mother. Adopted as a baby by a couple from Boston, now both deceased, all Bridget knew was that her biological mother had some connection to Magnolia Harbor.

A couple of weeks ago, while reading about South Carolina life in the nineteenth century, she'd learned that strawberries were an important crop during that era. When she next found out that Magnolia Harbor was celebrating a strawberry festival, it felt like fate was nudging her to visit. Her husband, Sean, a high school teacher, supported the idea, and here she was.

Butterflies beat in Bridget's belly. Would she find her mother? Maybe she was still living here in town. How would she react upon learning she had a grown daughter who wanted to meet her?

"Family research?" Grace asked, which sent the butterflies into overdrive. Had she guessed Bridget's purpose? Bridget studied her kind face, the warm eyes regarding her. They were only mildly curious, she decided. The innkeeper was merely making polite chitchat.

"No, for a book," Bridget said, squelching the dismay she felt at fibbing. Though it was only half a lie. "I'm planning to set a novel here in Magnolia Harbor."

Grace's brows rose. "What kind of novel?" She sounded genuinely interested.

"It's a romance, set in a small South Carolina town in the late 1800s. My main character is a lively young woman named Annabelle who falls in love." Bridget laughed. "That's all I've got so far. Somehow I'll end up with a book in a few months. It's a miracle every time."

The innkeeper smiled. "It sounds like you have a good beginning." She pointed to a rack of brochures. "There are a few historic sites in town you might want to check out. Plus we have a great library with an extensive local history collection."

Bridget's pulse beat faster at hearing about this potential treasure trove. Good historical details made books richer. "Thanks, I'll do that." She grabbed a guide to the town before following Grace upstairs.

"I've put you on the third floor," Grace said. "In the Wisteria Loft Suite. I hope you don't mind two flights of stairs."

Bridget, who huffed a little while trudging behind her trim hostess, managed to say, "No, it's fine. I can use the exercise." The downside of being a writer was the sedentary lifestyle. Recently Bridget had started writing while standing up. The first day was hard but she'd gotten used to it. Maybe the inn stairs helped Charlotte stay so trim. Not only was she a writer, she was a chef. Surely she had to sample all those delicious dishes she invented.

"This was totally worth the trip," Bridget said when they entered the Wisteria Loft Suite. The room wasn't huge but it was incredibly charming, with antique furniture and a fireplace. A French door led to the veranda.

Drawn as if by a magnet, Bridget dropped her tote and went to the doors. She stepped outside into the warm day and gazed at the lake view. Perhaps Annabelle should have a room like this. Maybe she should live in a house based on this inn.

Grace poked her head out. "Are you all set?" At Bridget's nod, she added, "If you need anything, let me know." With a final smile, she left.

Bridget found a pad and pen in her tote and returned to the veranda, where she plopped onto a wicker lounge chair. She'd work for a while, then give Sean and her fifteen-year-old daughter, Molly, a call. They'd be home from school just after four o'clock.

First, she jotted down the thoughts she'd had while driving through town, so she wouldn't lose them. Then she allowed herself to just be, to take in the sights, sounds, and aromas of this place. Using brief phrases, she described the sensory details as best she could. She could always look at photographs again—and she'd take plenty of those—but how else would she remember the scent of jasmine or the feather-light touch of a Southern breeze?

She had a lot here to work with for her book. But as her fingers went to her necklace, she realized how daunting her primary mission was. She had only the locket, which was engraved "Lula," and the knowledge that like Annabelle, her origin was here, in this town.

Grace

"I like the couscous," Grace said, setting down the sample plate. "Though I wouldn't mind having the chicken for dinner sometime."

Charlotte picked up the dish and rinsed it. "Bridget and Winnie agree with you, so that dish will move on to the next round." She added the plate and fork and silverware to the dishwasher.

"You're treating this like a mini contest." Grace smiled at her sister's methodical approach as she opened the refrigerator and pulled out the pitcher of tea. "She's all checked in, so that's the last for a few days. Full house." After pouring a glass, she studied the week's menu posted on the fridge. At six o'clock every night they hosted a wine and cheese social. Tonight they were doing a cheese and fruit platter, featuring strawberries of course. Blueberries, cantaloupe, and grapes completed the fruit selections. They were also offering brie, a locally sourced goat cheese, and sliced Vermont cheddar. Fresh shrimp cocktail and baked sausage canapés would round out the choices.

"I noticed Spencer came by earlier," Charlotte said, sending Grace a teasing glance. "What was he up to?" Spencer Lewis was their neighbor, having recently purchased Blossom Hill Farm nearby. The former FBI intelligence analyst and widower had become Grace's good friend.

Grace feigned surprise. "You saw him? I thought you were busy in here."

Charlotte wiggled her brows. "You can't hide anything from me, sister, so don't even try." Although the pair was more than a decade apart in age, they were close, each other's allies and best friends as well as business partners.

"He asked me—as a friend—to the dinner dance the last night of the festival." Grace smiled, looking forward to the event. "And I don't have a thing to wear."

Her sister whirled around and pointed a finger. "Shopping trip." Her mouth lifted in a lopsided smile. "Guess who asked *me* to go. He said we need to keep an eye on the competition."

Grace snorted. "That's easy. Dean. Maybe all four of us can go together."

Charlotte laughed. "Got it in one. Anyway, I need a new dress too." She wrinkled her nose. "But it won't be red or white or green. I'm already tired of those colors and it's only day one of the Fest." She shut the dishwasher door.

"I hear you about the strawberry colors. But don't forget, we're hosting a strawberry social tomorrow afternoon."

"I remember." Charlotte rolled her eyes. Then she clapped a hand to her head. "I spoke too soon. Our farm supplier brought by a tray and I forgot all about it. Until now." She marched down the back hall, to the area where deliveries were left.

Grace smiled at her sister's exasperation, knowing that in actuality, Charlotte thrived on a jam-packed schedule. So did Grace. They were doing work they loved and enjoying every minute of it.

Curt was the first to arrive for the social on the back veranda. He looked fresh and handsome in an open-necked shirt, track lines from a comb through his hair.

"White or red?" Grace greeted him.

"White, please." He moved to the canapés and made his selections, placing them on a small plate. "I took one of the kayaks out this afternoon and spent some time watching the ducks play around. I spotted several different kinds." He named the species.

Grace handed him the wine glass. "We have a lot of birds in Magnolia Harbor. Some of our birdwatcher guests even make lists, for fun." She wondered if he'd gotten in touch with Presley yet but didn't want to pry.

Davis and Anne Montgomery wandered onto the veranda, looking around. Both had changed their clothing, and Anne's blonde updo was neatly pinned into place. Spotting the food and drink set up at one end, they headed that way. Anne walked slightly behind her husband, Grace noticed. Her shoulders were slumped and a crease sat between her brows.

A stab of sympathy touched Grace's heart. Something was wrong. Was it illness? Or marital problems? Most couples who stayed at the inn exuded joy and happiness. Not this pair, although Davis didn't appear troubled. Grace said a silent prayer, asking God to bless her guest and help her with her troubles, whatever they were.

"Good evening," Davis said. "How are y'all doing?" He rubbed his hands together in delight as he regarded the spread. "Oh my. I bet that shrimp is fresh off the boat." He chose several from a bed of ice. "So many delicious choices."

"And look at those strawberries. They're gorgeous," Anne said. She pointed to the white wine. "I'd love a glass of that."

"Me too, thanks," Davis said. He filled a plate with strawberries, shrimp, cheese, and crackers, then prepared another for Anne under her direction.

Grace smiled at this courtly gesture. Hopefully his attentiveness would ease whatever was bothering Anne.

The Montgomerys introduced themselves to Curt, then wandered off to sit on wicker chairs near another couple. The foursome was soon chatting happily, but Curt lingered near Grace, giving her the distinct feeling that he wanted to talk privately to her. But before he could say a word, Bridget O'Brien appeared, a notebook tucked under her arm. Like Anne, she was frowning. Another worried guest? Hopefully the inn would work its healing magic and ease her anxieties.

But Bridget's face cleared when she saw the innkeeper. "Hi, Grace. I had the best afternoon working on my book." Hers was a frown of concentration, then, Grace realized with relief.

"A book?" Curt laughed. "Sounds intriguing."

Bridget pointed to the red wine in response to Grace's offer of red or white. "I hope so. It's a romance, set in a town much like Magnolia Harbor." She smiled at Grace. "I'm using this house as my model. It's perfect for my heroine to live in."

"How exciting." Grace handed her the wine. "Feel free to wander around any of the public areas." Bridget picked out a selection of cheese and crackers then drifted to the far end of the veranda. After she got settled, she opened her notebook and began to write.

Curt took a step toward Grace, but then Charlotte bustled out of the house, wearing an apron around her waist. "How are we holding out?" She checked the table expertly, rearranging a couple of items. "Looks good." The doorbell rang as the chef was walking toward the door. "I'll get it."

A minute or two later, she was back, a young couple accompanying her. The woman was petite, with long chestnut hair and bangs. Her companion was tall, with an insolent slouch and black hair combed back in a pompadour.

"Hey, Curt," the young woman said. "I know we're a little earlier than we planned."

Curt set his wine glass down on the tray for used dishes. "That's okay. I'm ready." He moved forward and gave the woman a tentative hug. "How are you, Presley?"

Presley patted his back. "I'm great. It's good to see you."

Grace gave the young woman a closer look. So this was the famous Presley. Curt extended his hand to her companion. "Hi, I'm Curt King."

The man returned his shake limply. "Hey. Presley's told me all about you. I'm Troy Cunningham, Presley's boyfriend."

5

Charlotte

Charlotte could tell by the expression on her sister's face—and Curt's—that meeting Presley's boyfriend was a surprise. The young doctor appeared to be tongue-tied, his gaze shifting between Presley and Troy. Even the socially adept Grace seemed stumped by the situation.

After a long, tense moment, Charlotte stepped in. "Where are you headed to eat?" she asked with a smile. "Professional curiosity."

"Charlotte is the chef here," Curt explained, finding his voice. He waved at the table of food. "As you can see, she does a fabulous job."

Presley exchanged a glance with her boyfriend, then said, "We're thinking of The Tidewater. The food is supposed to be good."

"Great choice," Charlotte said. "The chef is a friend of mine."

"Let's get going then." Troy pulled out keys and gave them a jingle. "Curt, do you want to ride with us or take your own car?"

Curt flinched, almost imperceptibly. "I'll take my car, thanks. Meet you there?"

The couple agreed and left. As soon as the inside door closed after them, Curt ran a hand through his hair and said, "Brother. I didn't see that coming."

Charlotte studied Curt with sympathy. "It's not over until they're married. Maybe she'll realize he isn't right for her. Be patient."

Curt shook his head, then said he wouldn't want to get between Presley and her boyfriend. He even made noises about staying in and forgetting about dinner.

Grace, who'd been listening, said, "I think you should go with Curt to The Tidewater, Charlotte." She raised her brows. "Check out the competition."

Charlotte didn't understand what her sister was referring to at first. Then she got it. "Oh, see if he's doing strawberry dishes? I'll bet he is. If we served dinner, I would definitely be testing them on our guests." She began to untie her apron. "Let me run and get changed and I'll go with you, Curt. If you don't mind."

For the first time since Presley had arrived and left, Curt's expression relaxed. "I'd really like that." He squared his shoulders. "It won't hurt my reputation a bit to be seen with you, Charlotte." He paused. "Strictly as friends, of course."

Charlotte bit back a smile. "Of course."

"Meet you out front in fifteen?" Curt asked, glancing at his watch. "I'm going to head to my room too."

Once he was gone, Charlotte gestured to Grace to step inside. "What's the story with Presley and Curt?"

Grace gave her the rundown, telling Charlotte how she'd encouraged him to contact her. "Now I feel terrible. Poor guy. That was quite a shock."

Charlotte tapped at her lip, thinking. "So when he called her, she didn't give him a heads-up she was bringing a date. I wonder why." Maybe Presley believed that she and Curt had truly moved on and it was entirely innocent. Another possibility was that she still had feelings for Curt, and flaunting her boyfriend was a way to gain the upper hand. Or to stir Curt's competitive instincts.

"Poor guy," Charlotte said, echoing Grace. "He seems too nice to fight for someone."

"At this point he has nothing to lose," Grace agreed. "Except maybe a little pride."

Charlotte hurried to her cottage on the grounds and took the fastest shower on record, not bothering to wash her hair. Then she slipped into a pretty top and black jeans, choosing a pair of black heels for her feet. She snatched up a small handbag holding her phone, keys, and a lipstick, and dashed back over to the inn.

Curt was seated on the front veranda, and he leaped up when he saw her on the path. "Thanks again for coming with me." His grin was a little sheepish.

Charlotte followed him to a black BMW sedan parked in front. "No problem. Dinner at The Tidewater will be a treat." In more ways than one. Hopefully she would be able to do a little covert investigation while she was there.

"I'll pay, of course." He opened the passenger door with a flourish. At her murmured protest, he added, "No, I insist. You're doing me a big favor."

At her direction, he turned left out of the driveway and headed toward town. The Tidewater was past the main downtown area, on the other side of the lake from the inn.

Curt mentioned that he'd bought two of Charlotte's cookbooks. "My mother is going to love the one on baking," he said. "And I'm enjoying looking through the one on easy meals. Perfect for a bachelor."

Charlotte laughed. "I'm so glad. The way to a chef's heart is through complimenting her recipes." The mention of the word *heart* gave her a lead-in to ask, "So what's the story with Presley?"

He kept his eyes on the road as he told her about their past relationship. "I was dumb to think that she'd still be available. Of course a woman as beautiful and lovable as Presley has men interested in her." Charlotte could see a muscle twitch in his jaw. "But when I scoped her out on social media, her status said she was single."

"Maybe the relationship is new," Charlotte suggested. "Or not very serious."

Curt held up crossed fingers. "Let's hope. I'm just not sure where to go from here." He shook his head. "I was so naive. I thought I'd swoop in, say I was sorry, and she'd fall into my arms."

Men were romantic dreamers too, Charlotte reflected. "All right. Let's think about plan B." She wracked her brain for a moment. "You said one of your big flaws in the past was being self-centered. Have you done anything to prove you've changed?" She held her breath waiting for his answer.

He tapped fingers on the steering wheel. "Does volunteer work with orphans in Haiti count?"

Charlotte smiled. "It might."

The parking lot of The Tidewater was nearly full, but Curt managed to squeeze into a spot near the Dumpster. "I guess a lot of people had the same idea to park back here," Curt said.

"Apparently so." Charlotte removed her seatbelt and opened the door, careful not to hit the metal container. "I'm sure a lot of diners are here because of Strawberry Fest."

Inside, a hostess greeted them with a warm smile. "Welcome to The Tidewater." She indicated a chalkboard by her podium. "These are tonight's specials."

Charlotte scanned them quickly while Curt told her they were meeting a group. *Strawberry-infused scallops . . . strawberry ceviche . . . blackened grouper with strawberry sauce.*

She was going to have to up her game, no doubt about it.

"Checking out the competition?" a familiar deep voice said behind her.

She spun around to see Dean bestowing his famous disarming smile. But despite the temptation to spill, she shook her head. "No,

I'm dining with friends." She gestured toward the hostess and Curt, who were waiting for her.

Dean rubbed his chin, stroking his perpetual five o'clock shadow. "I see. Well, enjoy. The scallops are quite good." With another quirk of his lips, he pivoted and headed into the dining room to make his usual rounds.

Hot prickles ran up Charlotte's spine. *He knew.* Dean had always had a sixth sense about what she was really thinking. Or hiding.

The hostess led them to the patio, one of the Tidewater's most beloved features. Enclosed by a stone wall, the brick-paved space was bright with standing lanterns and candles on the tables. Part of the patio was covered, but the hostess led them to a table out in the open where a group of six was seated. All the heads turned as one as Charlotte and Curt approached. Two remaining chairs were at one end, and the hostess seated them, Curt at the end of the table and Charlotte to his right.

Introductions went around, and Charlotte took note of the names. Denise, Micah, Cherish, Justin. All of them lived and worked locally, so she hoped they would remember her and recommend the inn to friends and relatives. Referrals were a big part of the inn's business.

As sweet tea was served and dinner orders were taken, and while listening to the general conversation, Charlotte secretly observed Presley and Troy. A lot of the exchange flew over Charlotte's head since it involved people she didn't know, past shared experiences, and inside jokes. Curt appeared equally lost, although he threw in an occasional one-liner that made everyone laugh. Presley kept glancing at him, her gaze by turns puzzled and something else . . . Thoughtful, Charlotte decided.

Points for Curt. A quick wit and sense of humor were very attractive traits. In contrast, Troy was a cynic, his comments revolving around how messed up work, the world, and life in general were. He was a pharmaceutical sales rep, and his skepticism even extended to his work.

Charlotte ordered the scallops. When the gorgeously arranged plate of pink-tinted seafood and Asian slaw was set in front of her, its savory aromas made her mouth water. For an instant, she fought down self-doubt. How could she beat this?

When she couldn't hold out any longer, she sliced off a piece of tender scallop with her fork. *Yum.* The seafood melted in her mouth.

"Do you like it?" Again that deep voice tickled in her ear.

She turned her head to see Dean behind her. He didn't seem to expect an answer, but smiled and nodded at the rest of the table. "How's everything, folks?" After they expressed murmurs of satisfaction and enjoyment, he said, "I'm Dean Bradley, your host and chef. We're delighted to have you join us."

After he sauntered away, Denise said, "It's always special when you meet the chef." She scooped a bite of the blackened fish. "I think it makes the food taste better."

"Charlotte is a chef," Curt announced, the first time he'd introduced a topic. "And a published cookbook author."

At their inquiring glances, Charlotte smiled and gave a modest overview of her career and present endeavors. "My books are available at the inn, at our local bookstore, and online of course."

"You were head chef at Le Crabe Fou in Charleston? I've been there," Cherish said. "It was so good." Others joined in with comments about the renowned restaurant.

"I'm glad you liked it," Charlotte said. "That's always nice to hear. But I have to say, I do admire people in the medical field. Cooking food versus saving lives? No contest." She smiled at Curt. "I was so impressed to hear about Curt's work with Haitian orphans."

As she hoped, the mention of orphans hit a home run. Denise and

Cherish jumped right in with questions, which Curt readily answered. His stories about the people he'd helped were heartwarming, and he downplayed his role with attractive modesty. Presley sat back and listened, seeming to concentrate on her meal. But Charlotte saw her repeated glances toward her ex-boyfriend. Mission accomplished. Or at least phase one.

6

Bridget

Chirping birds woke Bridget early the next morning. Oh, they had birds in Boston, but nothing as loud and determined as this gang. She rolled off the wonderfully comfortable mattress and padded to the curtains, pulling them wide.

Puffy clouds floated in a tender blue sky still tinted by sunrise. Fishing boats, kayaks, and canoes made trails across the glassy lake, but otherwise not a soul was in sight.

Bridget stepped out onto the veranda, enjoying the fact that she was perfectly comfortable in her pajamas. At home she'd need a sweater or jacket this time of day, even if it was May.

A door opened below, and Winston trotted out to sniff around the bushes and flower beds. Then he yipped in excitement and gave chase to a pair of squirrels, who bounded across the grass and up a tree smothered in blossoms. A magnolia tree, she realized. The white flowers were huge, larger than dinner plates, and they made a breathtaking sight against the glossy dark-green foliage.

What luck, to see the town's namesake tree in bloom. She'd definitely have to include magnolia trees in her book. Perhaps Annabelle could sit under one, reading a love letter.

Her belly gurgled, demanding food. Last night she'd been tired so she'd only grazed on appetizers instead of going out to dinner. Hopefully breakfast started soon. She couldn't remember what time Grace had said.

Sean's distinctive ring pealed on her phone and Bridget hurried inside to answer. "Hi, sweetie," she said. "Or should I say *hey*, now that I'm in the South?"

"Either, as long as you pick up when your lonely husband calls." His laugh was a deep, rolling rumble that immediately made her homesick. Her burly husband was good-humored and wise, a great partner and father, and an excellent teacher. He taught English at the high school their daughter attended.

"How's it going?" he asked. "Getting inspired?"

If there was one thing she totally adored about her husband, on top of all his other wonderful traits, it was his support of her writing. Some of her writer friends had spouses who wouldn't even read their books.

"Magnolia Harbor is fantastic." Bridget began to pace around the room, her habit while on the phone. She described the town and the inn, and gave him a brief overview of the plot that was percolating. With every word, the knowledge that she was hiding half the story of her visit grew into a bigger rock in her belly.

She and Sean had always been honest and open with each other—until now. The good communication they shared was something she cherished.

At her last doctor's appointment, she'd been diagnosed with high blood pressure. The condition was often inherited, the doctor said. This time when they asked about family medical history, her lack of knowledge struck her forcibly. She hadn't a clue whether her biological parents or grandparents had had high blood pressure, or any other conditions that might crop up, for that matter.

Molly had a right to know too. This fact, even more than her own health, made Bridget determined to try to open her closed adoption.

But with the high probability of failure, she had decided to carry out the investigation alone. If she hit a brick wall, Sean and Molly would never need to know. Even if she succeeded, there was no guarantee her birth family would want to meet her. No, it was better she do this on her own, for now at least.

"What was that, Sean? Sorry, I drifted off there a second." Bridget realized she'd been staring into space, fiddling with the locket.

Sean chuckled, unfazed since she often did that. "Thinking about your book? Molly wants to say hello. Then we have to fly or we'll be late for school."

After she talked to Molly, who was at the stage where her parents had to pry information out of her, Bridget hopped into the shower. According to the guest book, breakfast was officially served at eight o'clock, but before then coffee, fruit, and pastries were available. Those would do, since she had always been an early bird.

But so many ideas came to her in the shower—as they did while driving, walking, and even doing dishes—that it was after eight by the time she made it downstairs. She'd hurriedly dressed, then taken notes before the elusive ideas and images fled.

Breakfast was served on the outside veranda on good days and this certainly qualified. As Bridget crossed the foyer, she spotted a petite older woman with blonde hair in front of the brochure rack.

"Good morning," the woman said with a wide smile. "Sleep well?"

Bridget halted. "I sure did. It was incredibly peaceful and quiet, until the birds started in." She laughed at the memory.

"They're as happy about spring as we are." The woman rearranged several of the brochures, adding new ones from a box. "I'm Winnie Bennett, Grace and Charlotte's aunt. They let me hang out here now and then."

"Nice to meet you, Winnie." Bridget introduced herself. "I'm on my way to breakfast." The tantalizing aromas of bacon, coffee, and eggs were drifting from the direction of the kitchen. Her belly rumbled again in anticipation.

Winnie looked thoughtful for a moment, ran her fingers along the edge of one of the brochures, then handed it to Bridget. "I highly recommend this museum."

The Jackson House Museum, the brochure read. *One of Magnolia Harbor's historic treasures.*

"Thanks. I'll check it out." Slightly puzzled by the gift, Bridget continued toward the veranda. Her first stop was the coffee station, where she filled a mug with steaming java.

Curt King was seated by himself at the table, a pensive expression his face as he dug into an omelet. He glanced up when she sat down opposite. "Good morning."

"Good morning to you." She peered at his plate. "That looks good."

He cut off another piece. "They'll make whatever you want."

"Wow. That's awesome." Bridget sipped her coffee. She'd been expecting a buffet, which would have been just fine, if last night's social was anything to go on.

Grace popped outside. "Good morning, Bridget. What can we get you?" She listed the choices. "We do eggs any way you want them. And there are several choices of cold cereal too."

The first item she mentioned had piqued Bridget's appetite. "I'll have the baked strawberry pancake, please, with bacon on the side." After Grace bustled out, she said, "When in Rome . . ."

Curt laughed. "Yes, everything is strawberries this week." He glanced up and looked over Bridget's shoulder. "Like that, right there."

Bridget swiveled in her seat to see a woman dressed as a well-known strawberry-themed doll, complete with frilly mobcap. When she saw them looking at her, she gave them a perky smile and wave. "Hello," she said. "Is this where we get judged?"

"Not by us," Curt said, clearly biting back a snicker.

Grace stepped on the veranda, carrying a fresh pitcher of juice. The sight of the costumed guest made her footsteps stutter. "Aren't you cute?" After a brief pause, she said, "I'm sorry to tell you this, but we're not an official costume judging station. The paper made a mistake."

The woman's face fell. "Really? Where do I go, then?"

The innkeeper gave her a couple of suggestions, then wished her well. "Your breakfast will be right out," she told Bridget.

"Great. I'm starving." Bridget laughed. "I didn't bother with dinner last night."

"I went to The Tidewater." Curt set his fork down and picked up his coffee.

Something about his expression made Bridget ask, "It wasn't that good?"

Curt shook his head. "No, the food was stellar." He studied Bridget's face for a minute, then said, "I was out with my ex-girlfriend and her date."

Bridget winced. "Ouch. How did that happen?" Grace brought in a tray and set the contents in front of her. The baked pancake filled the plate, swimming in strawberries and butter. Grace also set down a pitcher of warm maple syrup. Smiling her thanks, Bridget picked up a piece of bacon and took a bite, savoring the salty crunch.

The doctor sighed, then launched into an explanation of the previous night's events. "I'm trying to figure out what to do now," he concluded. "I might check out and go home."

"Without talking to her? Nuh-uh." Bridget poured syrup on the pancake. "You really have no idea what's going on with her and Troy." Something panged when she heard her own words. She wasn't being exactly transparent, either. Maybe people in Magnolia Harbor might help her identify her mother, come up with a name, perhaps even know where she lived. But she wasn't quite ready to put that to the test.

"I suppose," Curt said. "But I think that inviting me to dinner and bringing her boyfriend sent a pretty clear message."

"But what message was it?" Bridget waved a hand. "Never mind. Not my business."

Curt glanced into his empty cup and got up. "Don't get me wrong. I appreciate your encouragement." He went over to the urn. "Grace and Charlotte have both been urging me to talk to Presley too."

"Well, there you have it." Bridget dabbed at her mouth with her napkin, then took another sweet fluffy bite. "The wisdom of women."

He sat down with his fresh coffee. "So tell me about your book."

There was a change of subject if she ever saw one. Bridget gave him the bare bones of the story she was developing. "This book is part of my Four Corners series. I'm writing historical romances set in the American Northeast, South, Southwest, and Northwest."

"That's impressive," Curt said. "I'll bet my mother would like your books." He set to work finishing the rest of his omelet.

"I can give you my card," Bridget said. "It has web addresses for my books online." She hesitated, then asked, "I have another question. If someone was looking for their biological parents in this state, where would they start?"

Curt thought about that. "I'm from North Carolina, which might have different laws." He grinned. "But I know someone who might be able to help you. She's an obstetrics nurse."

7

Anne

S*o far, not so good.* Anne pulled a pair of sunglasses over her eyes as she followed Davis to their car. The hour-long call between Davis and his mother the previous afternoon had squelched any further reconnecting activities, like the romantic stroll across the beautifully kept grounds and down to the lake she'd been hoping for. As Anne waited, self-exiled to the veranda so she wouldn't have to listen, every bad memory involving Cora had surfaced.

The first encounter had been at the country club, where the matriarch had glanced over her shoulder as if to locate her son's "real" date. The insincere performances at the engagement party and later at their wedding, Cora's teeth gritted the entire time. The ongoing lectures about what was suitable, acceptable, and expected—and her assumption that Anne didn't know proper social behavior.

But Anne loved Davis and knew he loved her, and that had carried her through the initial animosity and conflicts. She had also naively continued to believe that she and Cora would form a bond, joined by their mutual affection for Davis and Austin.

No such luck. As Anne opened the passenger door, she felt certain now that Cora would preside happily over the demise of her marriage. It would only prove what she'd not-so-secretly believed all along: Anne wasn't good enough for her precious baby boy.

"Shall we head downtown and walk around?" Davis asked from behind the wheel. "We can find someplace for lunch."

"Sounds good." Anne buckled her belt. Her enthusiasm was nil, and that must have shown because Davis sent her a sharp look.

"Maybe we'll find a nice piece of art," he said. "And I'll buy it for you as an early Christmas gift." Davis couldn't care less about art so Anne recognized the offer as an olive branch.

Anne patted the flyer about the festival. "There are supposed to be artists there, so yes, maybe we will." She tried to inject positive energy into her tone. She took a deep breath, sending a silent prayer heavenward. It might take a miracle to resolve their issues. She'd known from the beginning that Cora and Davis were close. Accepting her mother-in-law's behavior over the years had been part of an unspoken deal. She had never risked forcing the issue, and she never would. Cora wasn't about to change and it wasn't fair to make him choose between the two women in his life.

When they got there, downtown was swarming with visitors enjoying the fest. A little pulse of excitement traveled along Anne's veins as she took in the lively scene. Who knew a humble if delicious fruit would spark so much interest? Of course, in her view, strawberries should be celebrated every day.

With all the visitors in town, Davis had trouble finding a spot to park. The public spaces along Lake Haven Road were taken. The downtown lots were full. They circled once, then twice.

"Try the side streets on the hill." Anne pointed to an intersection. "Take that right." He obeyed, sending her a curious glance but thankfully not questioning her knowledge. She bit her lip. She'd better be careful or he'd guess the truth. And she wasn't ready for that.

You'd better get ready, that little voice said. *The day of reckoning is coming . . .*

Anne swallowed hard, trying to force the thoughts away. When Davis turned and eyed her, probably wondering if something was wrong, she said, "I just realized we're going to be doing a lot of walking. But the exercise will do me good."

Davis drove slowly up the side street. "You ought to go golfing with me. It would be fun, and that's exercise, especially when we don't use the carts."

Yes, an exercise in frustration. Anne had tried, but her lack of coordination meant she rarely connected club to ball. She sent more clods of turf flying than balls. "There's a parking lot," she said instead of replying. The golfing debate between them was a long-standing one.

This lot, three or four blocks from the lake, was only half full. Davis slid into a spot under a tree, another blessing. They parked, gathered their things, and began strolling down to the lakefront.

With each step, a memory rose up. As a child, Anne had explored every inch of this small village, either on foot or bicycle. Back then children were allowed to roam around, watched over by all the adults in town. She'd gone fishing in a little creek that emptied into the lake. Climbed trees and made playhouses in the middle of thickets. Absolutely lived in or on the water all summer long, with Lisa and their other friends.

What happened to me? Anne halted on the sidewalk. When and why had that joyous, energetic girl become a reserved, melancholy middle-aged woman?

She knew the answer. The day she'd left Magnolia Harbor.

"Are you tired?" Davis asked. "It's hot out here." A brimmed cap shaded his face and his eyes were covered by sunglasses. Overhead, the sun glared down and the first insects began to whir.

"I'm fine," Anne said. "Can't walk fast in this heat, that's all." Like an apparition, she glimpsed her girlhood self laughing and dancing her way down the sidewalk. Nothing had slowed her down then.

The discomfiting idea that someone might recognize her flitted through her mind, but was quickly dismissed. When she'd left she'd been a girl of seventeen. Now she was a woman in her middle years, a little plumper and with hair colored and highlighted to cover the gray. Some days she didn't even recognize herself in the mirror. It wasn't likely someone else would, especially since no one knew she was here.

They took a detour down Main Street, enjoying the shade cast by the tall storefronts. Here Anne found more changes in Magnolia Harbor. The buildings were the same but the businesses occupying them were far different, reflecting the times. Instead of matronly fashion emporiums there were cute boutiques. A former department store now held a variety of small enterprises. Farther down the street, The Book Cottage and Dragonfly Coffee Shop were both especially charming and inviting.

"I'd like to come back and browse through the bookstore," Anne said. "And then sit and read while drinking coffee at a sidewalk table."

"Sure thing." Davis took her hand, imitating the other couples strolling the cobblestone street. "Maybe when I'm playing golf." He made a mock wince as though expecting her wrath.

Anne laughed. "That works for me." She knew from experience that if he did go into the bookstore with her, she would feel compelled to rush. And hurrying and bookstores did not go together.

They held hands all the way down to the waterfront park, where booths crammed the park. Aromas of sausage, popcorn, and french fries filled the air.

"I feel like I'm gaining weight just breathing in," Anne joked.

Davis squeezed her hand. "You're beautiful, Anne. Just the way you are."

A rush of warmth that had nothing to do with the sun flashed over her. She felt like those petunias over there soaking up water from a gardener's hose. Refreshed. Infused with new life. How long had it been since her husband had complimented her?

"Thank you, Davis," she finally mumbled. "I'm glad you feel that way."

He gave her a final squeeze and dropped her hand, needing to walk separately in the throng. They strolled along the lines of booths, stopping now and then to admire the crafts or try samples of locally made foods. Several vendors were selling paintings. Anne admired several bright coastal scenes by an artist named Angel Diaz. She'd circle back and make a decision later.

"Let's go listen to the band and have some lunch," Davis suggested. A short distance away, a bluegrass band was crooning and picking next to Bobby's BBQ stand.

One of her husband's passions was fresh barbecue so Anne readily agreed to that plan. They made their way to a picnic table. "You wait here and I'll go buy," Davis said.

"All right. I'll have pulled pork and cole slaw. No bun." Anne gratefully accepted a seat in the shade, content to people-watch while her husband got in line.

Feeling delightfully anonymous in her wide-brimmed hat and shades, she scanned the crowd. All ages were attending the festival but she especially enjoyed watching the small children scamper around, eating ice cream cones or dancing on the grass to the music. Hopefully Austin would get married soon and give them grandchildren. The doctor from the inn, Curt, strolled by, arm in arm with Presley. They looked happy together, which was nice. She must have broken up with the other young man—or at least Anne hoped Presley had done the right thing.

"Why, I can't believe my eyes." Anne turned at the words to see a woman dressed in capris and a tank top standing nearby. Like many women her age, this one had beaten back time with a youthful teased hairstyle, lots of makeup, and bright polish on her fingernails and toes. Sunglasses covered half of her face.

"Can I help you?" Anne asked. Her heart began a slow, thudding beat. Was it possible she knew this person?

The woman took a step forward, pushing bangles up her arms then letting them fall with a clatter. "Don't you recognize me?" She stabbed a finger at her chest. "Nancy Higgins. Well, I was Nancy Blackstock."

Nancy Blackstock. The most popular girl in their high school class. She had worn her hair in a flip back then too, Anne remembered, and tossed her head the very same way, with arrogant pride.

"Hey, Nancy." Anne deliberately made her tone discouraging. She glanced toward the food booth, hoping that her old friend would leave before Davis got back. She didn't see him. Maybe he'd gone to the restroom or something.

But Nancy stepped even closer. "We always wondered what happened to you." Anne felt like covering her ears and humming until Nancy went away.

"Here we are, darling." With a sigh, Davis set a tray holding paper plates and drink cups on the table. "I had to circle around the crowd to get here in one piece."

"Who's this?" Nancy asked, her bangles clanking as she thrust out a hand. "Hi, I'm Nancy Higgins."

"Davis Montgomery." Davis shook her hand and gave Anne a confused look.

"We went to school together," Nancy said, pointing a finger between Anne and herself.

Anne wanted to curl up and die. She hunched her shoulders and stared at the picnic table, hoping and praying the interfering old bat would go away.

"Oh, at Tecumseh High?" Davis asked. Anne had created a history for herself, claiming that she grew up in a small town across the state. A town where, conveniently, she didn't have a friend or relative living.

Nancy cocked her head. "Tecumseh? No, Harbor High School." She pointed. "Right down the road."

Davis drew his brows together. "Oh. Nice to meet you, Nancy." He sat at the table and rubbed his hands together. "I'm starved." He reached for a french fry.

Girding herself, Anne turned in her seat to face her old friend. "Maybe we'll see you around this week, Nancy." She gestured at the food. "We both have low blood sugar so . . ."

Nancy put up both hands. "I'll leave you be, then. Enjoy your lunch."

Once Nancy retreated, Davis said, "Anne, what was that about? Neither of us have low blood sugar."

Heat burned in Anne's core, the mouthful of tender, tangy pork turning to ash. "I was trying to get rid of her gracefully."

Davis chewed, his jaw working. Even behind his sunglasses, Anne sensed his eyes boring into her face. "Anne. What's going on? What did she mean, you went to school here?"

Anne set down her fork, hit by a tidal wave of tangled, churning emotions. Here it was, the moment she'd dreaded—and tried to fend off—for decades.

"I lied," she finally whispered. Her lips quivered so she pressed a napkin to her mouth. Her puny wall was crumbling, washing away piece by piece. "I lied about everything."

His features collapsed and for a moment Anne saw what he would look like as a very old man. "I don't understand."

She bent her head, unable to stare at the wreckage she'd caused. "I couldn't—I couldn't tell you." Tears pooled in her eyes, dripped onto her legs. She felt weightless, insubstantial, a piece of flotsam carried along into the void.

He waited, his gaze lying heavy on her, hot like the sunshine. As the moments passed, a sense of panic-tinged urgency spiraled up inside her.

I have to tell him something, even just a little bit, take the first tiny step.

She inhaled and held the breath, trying to ratchet up her courage. She lifted her head. "Davis, I'm so sorry. I didn't mean for you to find out like this." Her mouth was dry, too dry to continue, so she took a sip of tea. "I grew up here, yes. And I left here, as a teenager."

Confusion filled his eyes. "But why was that a secret? I don't get it."

Anne stared at him. Once again the tidal wave crashed, a hurricane wind howling in her ears. She wasn't brave enough to say it all, to confess all her mistakes. He'd reject her and rightly so. So she gave him only the tip of the iceberg. "Davis, you have a loving family. I didn't. So I left. I had to."

He stuttered out a few questions, but Anne sat mute, unable to say more. Finally he stood, gathering his meal and trash with hasty hands. "Let's go. I'll drop you off at the inn."

"What are you going to do?" Anne asked, her insides shaking. She braced herself for the worst.

"I'm going to play golf, try to clear my head." His eyes were flinty, a cold anger she'd rarely seen lurking in their depths. He shook his head. "I thought we were better than this, Anne. I feel like I don't even know you."

A hollow sorrow filled Anne's chest. What she had always feared had come to pass. Telling the truth about her past meant losing her husband's love.

8

Bridget

After being informed by Grace that downtown parking was jammed due to the festival, Bridget got on the shuttle in front of the inn. She preferred that anyway, since her hands were free to take notes and her mind could safely wander. In the tote along with her notebook and camera were a town map and the brochure for the Jackson House Museum. She wore comfortable sneakers, capris, a cap-sleeved T-shirt, and slathers of sunscreen on her Boston-pale skin.

Bridget was ready to research, as she called her preliminary work on novels.

The shuttle made a couple of stops on the way downtown, with more people getting on than off. By the time they arrived at the festival, the shuttle was packed full, with passengers seated hip to hip and a baby drooling on Bridget's shoulder. She didn't mind. The poor tyke's face was beet red under her bonnet, and her mother didn't look much cooler.

"It's gonna be a scorcher," the young woman said, smiling at Bridget. A folded stroller rested against her knees and a bulging diaper bag sat at her feet.

"I'll say." Bridget fanned herself with the brochure Winnie had given her then put it back into her tote. She didn't mind the heat and the humidity, but didn't know if it was because she froze most of the year up north or because she had Southern blood.

Southern blood. That was a novel thought. Maybe she'd lived in exile all these years, away from her people. She regarded the friendly bunch chatting as the shuttle lurched along. The older man with his paunch and Clemson cap, his cuddly wife giggling at everything he said. The well-groomed young family wearing Bermuda shorts and polo shirts, each holding a phone. The adorable boy and girl kneeling on the seat, pointing out sights to their older siblings. Maybe it was a cliché, but Southerners did seem to be friendlier and more hospitable than people in other places.

Bridget smiled as her shoulders dropped in relaxation. For a few days, she was going to let herself unwind, to absorb the warmth of Magnolia Harbor, both literally and figuratively.

She disembarked with the other passengers in the heart of the festivities, then hesitated. Where to first? In a few hours, she was meeting Curt and Presley at the barbecue stand, which she could see over by the bandstand.

The library, she decided. Consulting the map, she saw it was on Willow Street, one block back from Main. She took the closest cross street, headed up a slight rise, and entered the historic district. Here the streets were cobblestoned, and the buildings a mix of brick storefronts and older homes, many of them now professional offices.

Trees filled with chirping birds shaded the street, and window boxes, gardens, and containers overflowed with flowers. Not a single building was taller than three stories high, and many had the false facades characteristic of the region.

Totally charming, was Bridget's verdict. She would have to bring Sean and Molly here sometime. Cheered by that thought, she quickened her steps, the brick library now in view. One of the Carnegies, she guessed by the tall arched windows and majestic entrance. A metal historic sign on the lawn bore her theory out, revealing that the structure had been built at the turn of the last century through the generosity of philanthropist Andrew Carnegie.

Taking a deep breath, she trudged up the marble stairs to the front door then entered air-conditioned comfort. Blinking her eyes to adjust after the sunlight, Bridget saw an older woman standing behind the semicircular desk straight ahead.

The woman looked up when the door swung shut behind Bridget, greeting her with a lift of her pointed chin. "How are you today?" she asked as Bridget approached, her attention half on her computer. "I'll be right with you." A strong Southern accent gave her words a lovely lilt.

Bridget looked around, noticing that she was the only patron in the library. That wasn't surprising with the festival going on a couple of blocks away.

"All right. How can I help you?" The woman patted her short gray locks into place, her blue eyes bright with intelligence and curiosity. A nameplate on the desk said *Phyllis Gendel.*

"I'm doing some research into local history," Bridget said. "For a book I'm writing."

Phyllis nodded. "You're not from around here, are you?"

Bridget laughed. "How could you tell? I'm from Boston, but I'm writing a romance set in a town like Magnolia Harbor." She pondered the research direction to take. "Do you have a local newspaper archive?"

The librarian began moving out from behind the desk. "We've got issues of the *Magnolia Times* and the *Harbor Gazette* on microfilm." Her gaze was questioning.

"I've used microfilm," Bridget said. "A lot."

"It's a dying art. Everything is gradually moving online." Phyllis gestured. "Come this way." She led Bridget to a room at the back, which she unlocked. "This is our local history room. We keep it locked unless someone wants to use it." She opened the door and stood back to let Bridget enter. "We've got a lot of rare materials in here."

Rare materials. Those words were like catnip to Bridget. She entered the room, inhaling the scents of old paper, leather, and wood, a blend that evoked libraries everywhere.

Phyllis went to a file cabinet and tapped on two drawers. "*Magnolia Times, Harbor Gazette*. The films are in here, organized by year." She pulled open the top drawer. "Which years are you looking for?"

Bridget had hoped to not reveal that, but she supposed that she'd better cooperate during her first visit to the library. She named a span five years before and after the date of her birth, not wanting to be more specific.

Phyllis dug out the right boxes and brought them over to a machine. While Bridget watched, she threaded the first one through, demonstrating how to use the films and monitor. "Anything you want to print, just press that button. Ten cents a page, pay up front." She watched for a minute to be sure Bridget understood everything, then excused herself.

As soon as the librarian was gone, Bridget inserted the roll dated the year she was born. Before spinning the dial, she took a deep breath, realizing that her palms were sweaty. She knew it was a long shot, but maybe, just maybe her birth was included in the announcements, even if her parents hadn't been married. She saw them all the time in her local paper now, listings that mentioned only the mother or an unmarried couple. But forty years ago? Maybe not.

Bridget barely took a breath as she searched the issues both before and after her birthday. The *Times* was a bust so she tried the *Gazette*.

The same result, meaning nothing. If only she had a name, she could search for her parents, find them mentioned in the newspaper, even in an obituary. She'd tracked down old friends that way. Obituaries often mentioned the current place of residence for each family member. Her gaze fell on a nearby shelf. Yearbooks from Harbor High School.

She was tempted to browse through them, but it might well be an exercise in futility since she didn't have either parent's name. And the student profiles almost certainly wouldn't reveal an unplanned pregnancy.

Bridget removed the film and rolled it up, then returned the boxes to the file cabinet drawers. She still had over an hour before she was supposed to meet Curt, so she thought she might as well do something for her book.

The Jackson House Museum, the one from the brochure Winnie had given her, was nearby. Touring the building would probably take just about the right amount of time, and she might even be able to use it, or some of its details, in Annabelle's story.

"Did you find what you needed?" Phyllis looked up from checking in books when Bridget entered the main room a few minutes later.

"I did, thank you," Bridget said, not wanting to get into any detail. "I'll probably be back to take another look at your historical collection."

"Any time we're open." Phyllis slid another book under the scanner. "Have a good day."

Bridget checked the hours posted on the door for future reference, then set out for the museum. It was just a couple of blocks away, so it should be easy to find.

The Jackson House Museum was located on a block of brick three-story homes and was built in 1806, according to the sign out front. Two brick pillars in a wrought iron fence marked the entrance to a stone path between small patches of lawn. Not much of a yard, but the enclosure gave the house a sense of privacy.

Bridget turned the brass handle ornamenting the shiny black door, only to have it pulled open from the other side.

Anne Montgomery put a hand to her chest. "Oh, you scared me."

"Sorry," Bridget said with a laugh. She stepped aside to let Anne exit. "How was it?"

The other woman cocked her head. "How was what?" Squinting

against the bright sunlight, she pulled sunglasses down from her hair.

"The museum," Bridget said. "Judging by the brochure, it's gorgeous."

Anne turned away. "Oh, it is. Well, I'd better be going. See you back at the inn." She hurried up the path to the street.

Shrugging at her fellow guest's abruptness, Bridget continued inside. The entrance hall wasn't large but it had high ceilings and a breathtaking cantilevered staircase.

A woman dressed in period costume stood near the door. "Isn't it lovely? That staircase goes up all three stories."

"Can I take a peek?" Bridget stepped across wide polished boards that creaked gently under her feet.

"Go ahead. If you want an official tour, we're starting in ten minutes. Otherwise poke around on your own."

Bridget liked the sound of the latter. She usually found it easier to absorb the atmosphere of a place when left to her own devices. As she stepped reverently across the hall, she took in the paneled wainscoting, carved plaster ornaments, and high-quality antiques.

She rested her hand on the polished banister and started up the curving staircase, imagining herself wearing clothing of Victorian vintage. As the staircase wound to the left, an enormous portrait of a woman high on the wall came into view.

By the hairstyle and clothing, Bridget guessed the portrait had been painted decades ago. Since she was alone on the staircase, she paused to take in the details. The woman was wearing a locket around her neck, heart-shaped like hers. Bridget pulled it out from under her top, sliding the silver bauble back and forth on its chain.

She compared her necklace to the one in the picture. They were almost identical in shape. No, they were *exactly* alike. Her heart began to thud, her subconscious picking up something her mind wasn't ready to acknowledge.

Too bad she couldn't get closer. Then she had an idea. She pulled out her camera and zoomed in on the portrait, making sure that she was going to capture a crisp, clear image with the telephoto lens.

Once she snapped the shot, she examined it. Despite the painting being over a century old, the name *Lula* was plainly visible on the locket.

9

Grace

"Remind me again why we agreed to do this," Charlotte grumbled. She removed beaters from the third big bowl of whipped cream she'd mixed so far.

Rows of glass dishes holding individual strawberry shortcakes lined the gleaming kitchen counter. "Because it's a fundraiser for children's summer programs." Grace hid a smile at her predictable sister's reaction. Charlotte had the habit of taking on too much at times and then regretting it. But once the strawberry social got started, she'd relax and enjoy it, all the hard work forgotten.

"When I suggested it to the chamber, I had no idea they would sell a hundred tickets," Charlotte said. "Good thing I ordered more strawberries."

The back doorbell chimed. "And there they are," Grace said. "I'll go get them." As she hurried to the door, she glanced down at her white bib apron. With all the strawberry juice spattered on there, she looked like she'd been injured.

Roy Bevins was waiting patiently at the back door, a tray of flats in his hand. "Here you are, Miss Grace. Glad I had enough for you. They're selling like hotcakes."

Grace took the tray from the older gentleman. "That's what we were hoping for, right? I'll make sure to tell everyone they came from your farm." The Bevins family owned a small organic farm on the outskirts of town. In addition to strawberries, they offered peaches, eggs, blueberries, and a variety of vegetables. The quality was always top-notch.

"I appreciate that. We can use all the marketing we can get." Winston barreled past Roy's feet and entered the back hall, making them both laugh. "Well, I'd best be on my way." The farmer tipped his battered hat. "Have a good day, you hear?"

"You too, Roy." Grace shut the door. Winston followed her to the kitchen, leaping and sniffing loudly, the way he did when he smelled something good. "These are strawberries, Winston, not treats."

Did dogs even like strawberries? Grace plucked a small fruit from the tray and dropped it onto the floor. With a snuffle, Winston gobbled it up, then looked around for more.

Grace laughed. "Who knew?" She carried the berries into the kitchen. "Guess what? Winston likes strawberries."

"Really?" Charlotte paused, then tasted a spoonful of whipped cream. "I guess we'd better keep an eye on him today." She shook her head. "And here I've been worried about bees and wasps, not our dog."

"He'll be good. Right, Winston?" Grace smiled at her adorable pet, who cocked his head and yipped in reply. Then she noticed the time. "Yikes. I'd better get moving." She foraged in the cupboard for the largest colander and gently dumped strawberries into it.

Charlotte set down her spoon in the sink then sprinted to the oven when the timer went off. "The last batch of biscuits is finally done."

Once the biscuits were cooled, the sisters worked together to assemble the rest of the desserts and to brew numerous pitchers of iced sweet tea. After the shortcakes went into the big refrigerator, Grace headed outside to cut flowers for the tables. She paused to survey the garden, which was ready for the event. The rental company had come earlier to set up canopies, tables, and chairs in shady areas. The dessert and cold drinks would be served on the veranda, and there was some seating there as well.

Out in the garden, Grace cut individual flowers with her snips and placed them in a flat basket. With a wide hat tied on her head and a pair of gloves protecting her hands, she felt like a lady of the manor working in her garden—which she supposed she was.

Her movements among the bushes were accompanied by fat, lazy bees climbing into the sweet blossoms. In keeping with the strawberry theme, Grace chose pure white roses as well as crimson ones. Many of the varieties were heirloom, planted a century ago and still blooming profusely. Creamy gardenias and calla lilies would round out the arrangements, she decided, as well as sprays of dark-green magnolia leaves.

"Grace. There you are." She looked up to see Curt coming across the lawn, Winston at his heels. "Charlotte said you were out here."

She selected another rose and clipped the stem. "How are you, Curt?"

He stood, hands in pockets. "Not bad. Presley is going to meet me later so we can talk."

"How did dinner go?" Charlotte had filled her in, of course, but Grace didn't want to tell him that. Besides, she wanted his impression, not her sister's, who was convinced Presley would soon ditch Troy for Curt if she hadn't already.

He looked thoughtful. "Okay. I wasn't impressed with her boyfriend. He's all wrong for her."

No doubt any other man would be, in the young doctor's view. "So she agreed to meet you?"

He paced about the bushes, pausing to cup a rose and smell it. "Yes. I was kind of surprised. But Charlotte said Presley warmed up to me over the course of dinner, so that gave me the guts to ask again if I could see her. Without Troy." He moved on to another flower. "Bridget is going to be there part of the time, which will hopefully help break the ice."

"Our Bridget?" Grace was surprised, although she'd seen Bridget and Curt talking at breakfast. "Why is that?"

His answer was vague. "She thinks Presley can help her with some local research."

Probably for her book. Grace supposed that writing a book entailed all sorts of inquiries into a number of topics. She glanced up at the veranda and saw Winnie placing silverware on the serving table. Good, she'd been able to come over and help. With the unexpected success of the fundraiser, they needed her.

"Is there anything I can do?" Curt asked, following her gaze. "I see you're getting ready for something."

"Yes, we're hosting a strawberry social." Grace didn't generally press guests into service but when she saw Winnie struggle to move a side table, she said, "If you could give Winnie a hand, that would be wonderful." *What a nice young man.* He'd already helped them with the bunting and now furniture arranging.

"Of course." Curt headed off across the grass toward the veranda, waving at Winnie and telling her to wait.

Grace finished cutting flowers and carted the overflowing basket to the house. In the pantry, she selected a number of vases in different shapes, then set to work making the arrangements.

Charlotte darted in and opened a big drawer holding linens. "I need another tablecloth. We had an accident with some iced tea. Winston may or may not have been involved."

Grace laughed. "We've got plenty, fortunately." They bought linens in bulk, mostly white so the fabric could be bleached and kept spotless. "What do you think?" She gestured at the flowers.

"Wow." Charlotte bent and smelled a crimson rose. "They're gorgeous." She grabbed one of the vases along with the tablecloth. "I'll put this out."

Grace was setting the last vases on the tables when Anne emerged onto the veranda. Beyond her hot and disheveled appearance her eyes held a haunted shadow and lines of sorrow creased her face. She didn't just look terrible. She looked bereft.

Alarm thrilled through Grace. What had happened? "Hi Anne," Grace said, keeping her tone light. "Did you have a nice time at the festival?"

Anne seemed to realize her hair was falling down and began to tuck it up. "Okay, I guess." Her voice was flat. "Davis wanted to play golf so I came back here."

Grace's heart twisted in sympathy for the couple, who were having problems, it appeared. "Why don't you join us? A strawberry social is starting in half an hour. Unless you want to just relax. It's a nice afternoon for a nap."

"Oh, a social sounds wonderful," Anne said. "I wondered what was going on when I saw the tables and flowers." She glanced around some more then said, "I'll run up to my room and shower." She pulled at her clinging top and attempted a smile. "It was really hot walking around town. Can you tell?"

"See you in a few." Grace hoped Anne *would* come down after showering. Members of The Busy Bees quilting group were attending and, knowing their kind hearts, they'd take Anne under their wing. She looked like she could use a few friends right now.

A short while later, the crowd descended and Grace, Charlotte, and Winnie were kept running serving the shortcakes and replenishing pitchers of beverages. Many of the female attendees had dressed for the occasion in wide-brimmed hats and pretty sundresses. Flitting around the lawn, their colorful beauty rivaled the flower gardens.

After everyone was served, Grace went around with an iced tea pitcher, a perfect opportunity to speak to those she knew and greet people she didn't. Anne, looking fresh in pink linen slacks and matching shell top, was seated under a tree with a couple members of The Busy Bees.

"This has been so much fun," Anne said to Grace. "I've been

talking quilting with Helen and Judith. I'm going to stop by Judith's shop soon so I can start a project."

Judith Mason, short and comfortably plump with flawless dark skin, adjusted her glasses with a smile. She owned Spool & Thread downtown. "I've been telling Anne about the baby quilt kits we've put together. Perfect for a grandchild."

Anne laughed. "I don't have one of those yet." She held up crossed fingers. "But I think Austin is going to ask his lovely girlfriend to marry him. I guess I'm jumping the gun a bit."

"No shame in that." Helen reached out and patted Anne's forearm. Judging by the crease between her eyes, Grace could tell it wasn't a good day for Helen, who suffered from rheumatoid arthritis. "I say go for it."

"I will." Anne's gaze was distant. "I'll have to pick colors that work for boys or girls, since who knows what they'll have." She smiled, but once again Grace saw a flicker of sadness and grief in her eyes.

Her guest was definitely struggling with something. Grace said a silent prayer that whatever it was, it would be happily resolved.

10

Bridget

Bridget strolled down the sidewalk toward the festival, barely noticing the lovely historic buildings she was passing.

Her mind was consumed with the locket, her only inheritance. After spotting the identical one in the portrait, she'd cornered the docent.

"Who is that?" she asked, pointing to the portrait. "What a marvelous painting."

The docent nodded. "It is. That's Olympia Jackson, painted in 1940." She named the artist. "He was quite famous in the South for painting portraits of wealthy patrons. It really belongs in an art museum but Olympia didn't want it to leave the premises." She waved a hand. "The same for all the furnishings, no matter how rare or valuable they are."

Had she felt the same way about her jewelry? There *was* a possibility that the locket had been given away, stolen, or sold. But by the sounds of it, Olympia Jackson had believed in hanging on to the family heirlooms, so she would proceed with the assumption it had belonged to Olympia and somehow had been handed down to Bridget. She tamped down the swell of excitement that tingled through her. This might come to nothing. Or everything. "Do you have any information on the Jacksons?" she finally asked.

The woman reached for a brochure, this one providing more information than the brief overview in the general museum one that Bridget already had. "This gives some details. The Jackson family was one of the most prominent in Magnolia Harbor. They owned a block of storefronts and also supplied mercantile businesses with goods from Europe, the Far East, and the northern states."

Bridget took the brochure and held it, her heart beginning to pound so hard she was breathless, her earlier attempt at remaining realistic gone. How astounding would it be if she found her answers within a day of her arrival? She took a deep breath before asking, "Is the family still around?"

But the docent shook her head. "Not that I know of. Olympia Jackson died about ten years ago and left this house in a trust."

Bridget sagged with disappointment. "That's too bad. How old was she?"

If the woman thought her question odd, she didn't say. "Oh, in her seventies, I think. I never met her. I only moved here last year." She smiled. "At least it's a good use of my history degree while I wait for a teaching job to open up."

Hope sparked anew in Bridget's chest. Maybe Mrs. Jackson had been her grandmother. On either side, she supposed, since the locket could have come from her father. Although why Mrs. Jackson's daughter or son wouldn't be involved with the museum, she had no idea. "There weren't any children to carry on the legacy, huh?"

The docent gave an open-handed shrug. "I guess not. But I've been focused on learning about the early generations. I could look into it for you, if you want, see if any relatives are still living."

Did she want that? Bridget couldn't think of a discreet approach. Then she did. "Maybe," she said. "I'm working on a book." That excuse seemed to cover a lot of bases, she was realizing.

"Oh, and you might want to talk to them?" The docent's eyes gleamed. "Let me know." She reached for a business card on the table. "I'm Becky Thomas."

Now, her mind whirling with thoughts, Bridget reached Lake

Haven Road and waited at the crosswalk to cross the road. Cars passing, the throngs of people, music from the bandstand—all hit her senses, remote and filtered as if she were watching a television show.

When a double stroller holding twin boys almost ran over her foot, she forced herself to wake up. She crossed the street and entered the park, winding her way between the booths. Curt and Presley were meeting her by the bandstand, where a country rock group was playing. Bridget paused under a spreading live oak and took a deep breath. She needed to put her speculations on hold and pay attention to this experience.

Sure, New England had fairs and festivals, but they didn't offer country rock bands belting out *Sweet Home Alabama*, boiled peanuts, and fried catfish with hush puppies. Bridget skipped the peanuts but, suddenly starving, purchased a plate of fish with macaroni and cheese, greens, and a hush puppy. And a cup of sweet tea too, of course.

Curt was sitting with an attractive young woman who Bridget thought must be Presley at a picnic table near the lake, tall to-go cups in front of them. Thankful she'd been given a tray, Bridget carried her meal down to the spot, doing her best to avoid the people milling around or lounging on the grass.

"Hey." Curt waved. "Glad you found us."

Bridget set her tray down, smiling at the young woman. "The festival appears to be a success."

"Sure does." The young woman smiled and extended a hand. "I'm Presley."

"Nice to meet you. I'm Bridget." She shook the nurse's hand. "It's so nice of you to meet with me." She smiled at Curt, thankful he'd thought to connect the two of them. By the fond looks he kept casting Presley's way, she guessed he cared for her a great deal. Hopefully Presley returned his feelings.

"No problem," Presley said. "I'm glad I can help. Or I hope I can, anyway."

Bridget picked up her fork. "I hope you don't mind if I eat. I didn't have lunch."

"No, go on." Curt studied her plate. "You got the catfish. Good choice."

"I've never had it before." Bridget took a bite, not sure what to expect. The fish was light but savory and slightly salty. The breading was nicely thin and crunchy, different than the thicker batter she was used to in New England. Next she tried a bite of macaroni and cheese, which melted in her mouth, buttery and rich. The greens were good too, livened up with a touch of vinegar. "Yum."

"We'll make a Southerner of you yet," Curt joked.

Bridget's heart lurched. Once again she experienced a strange sense of dislocation. If her parents had kept her and raised her in South Carolina, catfish wouldn't be a novelty. But would she *ever* have eaten those slimy nuts bubbling in a vat of hot water? "I think I'll skip the boiled peanuts, though."

Presley laughed. "They're actually good, once you get past the idea of the wet shells."

"I'll take your word for it," Bridget said.

The couple looked at each other, then Curt said, "You wanted some information about adoption, right, Bridget?"

Bridget set her fork down. "Yes, about how it's handled in South Carolina, specifically in a small town like this."

Presley nodded. "I have seen a few adoptions in my work as a delivery room nurse, although more women keep their babies than a few years ago—or at least that's what my older colleagues at the hospital tell me. Being a single mother doesn't have the stigma it used to." She picked up her drink and sipped through the straw.

If that had been the case when she was born, would her mother have kept her? Bridget hoped so. "Are they usually open adoptions?" That was another regret, that her records were sealed.

"I wouldn't say usually, but often," Presley said. "I think it's great that more adoptive parents keep the birth mother involved." Her eyes grew thoughtful. "It must be so hard to give up a baby and never see him or her again."

"I can't imagine it," Bridget said fervently. "I fell madly in love when my Molly was born." The very idea of relinquishing Molly to strangers made her queasy. How had her mother done it?

"You have a daughter?" Curt asked politely.

For a couple of minutes, Bridget filled them in on her family and life in Boston. Then she returned to the topic of adoption. "So, if someone had a closed adoption but wanted to find their birth family, what could they do?" Her heart thumping in anticipation, she set aside her tray and pulled out her notebook.

Presley sighed. "The short answer is, it can be complicated. Sometimes even impossible."

Bridget's hopes sank but she tried to hide her consternation. "How so?"

The nurse sighed again. "Now, remember, I'm no expert but I went through this with one of my friends. She was adopted back in the 1980s."

"A little later than . . . my book." Bridget caught herself. "But that will work. Was she successful?" She held her breath, waiting for the answer.

"Eventually." Presley folded her straw paper into a tiny square and Bridget had to hide a smile. Molly did that exact same thing. "It took a couple of years."

"Oh my. That's terrible." Bridget couldn't hold back the exclamation.

When they looked at her in surprise, she added, "I'll have to shorten the timeline in my book, to fit the rest of the plot." *And hopefully my personal timeline will be shorter too.* Bridget didn't know if she had the patience or fortitude to wait that long. She was one of those people who, once they made a decision to try something, wanted to see results right away.

Presley pulled the folded paper open, revealing an accordion shape. "You have to work with the adoption agency for everything. That's what takes so long. All the requests need to go through them."

"So you'd start by writing to them?" Bridget inquired. The name of the agency was in her papers somewhere. She hadn't yet had the courage to check to see if they were still in business, but now that she'd set the process in motion, she would.

"Yes. They are usually willing to release nonidentifying information about the birth family, but even that can take a year."

"What's included in that?" Curt asked.

Presley folded the straw paper again. "If you're lucky, you'll get information about the birth parents, their ages, medical history, occupations, education, that kind of thing."

Bridget felt a small pang of relief. A desire to learn her family medical history had launched this quest, and maybe she'd at least get that. But now she hoped to learn more, she realized, much more. She wanted to know about their lives since her birth, where they had gone to school and what their occupations were. If they had other children—meaning she had siblings. That was a big one. She yearned for the tiny details too, the little facts people took for granted about each other. Maybe her mother liked catfish and tapped her feet to country rock.

"My character wants to meet her birth mom," Bridget said, a surge of determination shooting through her core. "So how does that happen?"

"The agency will contact the birth parents, if they can find them, and see if they're agreeable." Presley pursed her lips. "If not, well it will be a dead end, I'm afraid."

Bridget rested her head on her hand. There it was, the biggest risk of all. She wasn't sure she could face the rejection. It was bad enough to be given away, even to a loving family. But to know for certain that your mother didn't want you in her life even now, over forty years later . . .

Presley reached for her phone. "There is one other possibility." She scrolled through several screens. "And you can thank the Internet."

Bridget raised her head. "What is it?"

"People post on this site." Presley handed her the phone. "There are websites for children looking for parents and vice versa. It's brought a lot of people together—including my friend with her birth parents. The agency was sitting on her file so she tried this."

Fingers trembling, Bridget scrolled through information about the registry. If she was brave enough to post her information, would her mother or father find her?

Maybe they were already looking.

Was she ready to take the biggest risk of her life?

11

Anne

"It was so nice to meet you," Anne told Judith and Helen. The straw-berry social had wound to a close and the guests were filtering away. "I'll be stopping by the shop to check out those baby quilt kits."

Upstairs in her room, Anne had debated coming back down, not sure if she wanted to face people. And what if someone else recognized her? But she'd taken the risk and found that spending time with new faces had provided respite and an easing of her painful thoughts.

"Please do come by the store." Judith winked. "We give our friends a nice discount."

Helen clasped her hand with gnarled fingers. "It was lovely to meet you, Anne. I hope to see you again before you go home."

Anne's heart warmed. These two wonderful women considered her a friend? She couldn't remember the last time she'd had such a pleasant afternoon, the conversation about nothing special but warm and even loving. Her thoughts flitted home to Charlotte, where she always felt on edge, as though every word and action was being judged.

Lovely, kind people lived in Charlotte too, of course. She'd just never had the good fortune to meet them. Her social circle was dominated by Cora and her mob of meddling matriarchs. Anne bit back a laugh at this description of her formidable mother-in-law. Perhaps she should poke fun more often at the absurdity of it all. Where had her sense of humor gone?

Maybe she'd left it right here, in Magnolia Harbor.

Anne said goodbye again, watching as the women made their way across the grass to the veranda. There they took leave of Grace and Charlotte, who were standing by the door into the house. Most of the guests were staying on the veranda to go around to the front, where they had parked. The beauty of a wraparound porch, she supposed. It saved traffic through the house.

The table under the tree still held a clutter of dishes, glasses, and crumpled napkins, so Anne began to pick them up and put them on a tray. She glanced up at the blue sky. Judging by the angle of the sun, Davis wouldn't be back for another hour or so.

Her belly clenched at the thought of her husband. He'd soon return, sunburned and expecting answers—which he had a right to do. How was she going to explain the secrets she'd kept? Davis wasn't perfect by any stretch, but if there was one thing she could count on, it was his integrity. His reputation for honesty had served him well in his business. He never shaded a number or slanted a financial statement, although he'd been asked to by less than scrupulous clients. Former clients now. The standard he'd raised had been another challenge in her life. One she'd failed miserably to reach, obviously.

"You don't have to do that," a voice at her elbow said.

Anne turned to see Grace. "I don't mind. In fact, I'd like to help. My way of saying thank you for a delightful afternoon."

Grace bent to pick up a stray napkin. "It did go well, didn't it? We were a bit worried when the chamber told us we were hosting a hundred people. We thought we'd have fifty, maybe."

"That is quite an increase." Anne stacked the silverware by itself, knowing that it would make the job of washing easier. "Figuring out how much food to make is always a challenge." Anne had hosted a number of parties herself. Buffets provided the most flexibility, she'd found. But Grace and Charlotte had needed to prepare individual shortcakes. "You were able to find enough strawberries, obviously."

"We have a wonderful farm where we buy a lot of produce. The owner came through for us." She glanced down at her feet, where Winston was snuffling around for stray crumbs. "I learned today that Winston enjoys strawberries too."

"I had a dog that liked them too," Anne said. "And peaches? Oh my. You couldn't leave your dish anywhere she could get at it." Here was another nice memory, preempting the ugly ones. Her childhood dog had been appropriately named Peaches. She'd been a good old girl.

The two women carted the dishes into the kitchen, where Charlotte was loading the dishwasher. "We should have used paper," the chef grumbled.

Grace began to rinse the etched-glass dessert bowls used for the shortcakes. "But these are so much prettier."

"They definitely added to the experience," Anne said. She threw away trash and heaped the dirty cloth napkins in a hamper used for that purpose. "The whole thing was lovely. And the shortcake? To die for."

Charlotte threw her a wide smile. "I'm glad you liked it. It's a special family recipe."

"Really?" Anne asked. "That sounds intriguing."

Grace rolled her eyes at her sister. "*Not* really. But maybe it is now."

"As of today it is," Charlotte declared. "I've decided to use it in my new cookbook, *Comfort and Cheer from Magnolia Harbor Inn*." She gestured gloved hands in emphasis. "Featuring simple but visually stunning and delicious dishes from appetizers to dessert. And lots of inn photographs too. We'll stage each shot."

"What a wonderful concept," Anne said. "I'll buy a copy and tell all my friends. Plus make sure my local bookstore carries it."

Charlotte's brows rose. "That's so nice of you. Thanks."

"I love the idea too," Grace said. "Did you come up with that today? During all the stress of putting together a hundred shortcakes?"

"A hundred and three," Charlotte corrected. "But who's counting? And yes, it popped into my mind while I was working my little fingers to the bone." She held up her hands, fingers spread. "For some reason I think better under pressure. But I guess that goes with being a chef."

Grace wiped the counters clean with a cloth. "I think we should start the cocktail hour a little early. What do you think, ladies?"

"I'm in." Charlotte pushed a full rack in and closed the dishwasher door. "There's not much to do since we're offering a cold collation tonight."

"Fancy," Grace teased. "Where did you get that term?"

"From a Victorian cookbook I'm reading." Charlotte pushed the wash button and the machine began to hum. "It means a light meal consisting of only cold food."

"Cold collation," Anne mused. "That sounds like something my mother-in-law would say." She felt her face twist into a wry expression. Cora would have been happier living a century ago, she often thought. Back when parents picked mates for their children.

Grace picked up the hamper. "Let me start a load of wash and then I'll meet you on the back veranda."

A few minutes later, glasses of wine in hand, the trio relaxed in wicker chairs and watched afternoon shade toward evening. They made casual chitchat—about the inn, the festival, Charlotte's anxiety about the entrée contest.

"After eating at The Tidewater last night, I've really got to up my game," Charlotte said. "Dean's food was sublime." She described the strawberry-infused scallops and the blackened grouper, which Curt had ordered.

"I liked your couscous recipe," Grace said. "It had asparagus and strawberries," she told Anne.

Charlotte leaned back against the cushion with a sigh. "I liked it too. But now I'm rethinking all my ideas. None of them are good enough."

Anne raised her brows, sending Charlotte a teasing look. The ease she felt with these women was surprising. And nice. "Why don't you let us be the judge? I'm more than willing to taste your inventions and give my honest opinion."

"Offer accepted." Charlotte slapped the arm of her chair then launched herself up and out. "Now I'd better get to work." She grabbed her empty wine glass. "And before you ask, I don't need any help. Cold collations are easy. That's the point of them, I think."

The other two remained where they were, enjoying the view of the lake, where a few boats buzzed along the glassy water. Anne sighed, feeling the remainder of her tension dissolve.

"That was a big sigh," Grace said with a sideways glance.

Anne laughed. "It was." She hesitated but felt only gentle warmth and caring from the innkeeper. Before she fully realized what she was doing, she said, "I had quite an upsetting day. Before the strawberry social, I mean."

Grace made an encouraging sound, her gaze focused on the view.

"My husband and I . . ." Anne dragged in a shuddering breath. "This trip was supposed to be like a second honeymoon." Tears burned in her eyes and for a moment, she couldn't speak.

"Don't talk if you don't want to," Grace said urgently. Her hand was soft and warm on Anne's arm.

Anne shook her head, swallowing the lump in her throat. "No, it's okay. It's just . . . some things came up. Kind of blew up out of nowhere, as they do." Thanks to Nancy's sharp eyes. "He's angry and I don't blame him a bit."

"Sometimes a cooling-off period can help," Grace said cautiously. "When people disagree."

"Yes, we do that all the time." That had been the pattern in their marriage, Anne realized. When they had an argument, which was rare, each would retreat to their corner for a while. Davis would run off to the office or golf course and Anne would clean the house or work in the garden, burning off volatile emotions.

Not this time. When Davis came back, he'd want answers.

And what was she going to tell him?

A small motorboat turned off its course and headed for the inn's dock. "I think you might have a visitor, Grace," Anne said.

Grace turned to look, shading her eyes with her hand. "Oh, that's Spencer, our neighbor. I wonder what he wants."

Davis appeared in the doorway. "I'm back." He obviously was trying to inject a teasing tone into his voice but it fell flat. Anne noticed that his usual air of confidence was missing, reflected in sagging shoulders and the uncertainty of his gaze.

The innkeeper jumped to her feet. "I'm going down to talk to Spencer. Here, Davis, take my seat. Fresh sweet tea is on the table." She crossed the veranda and stepped down onto the lawn.

Anne appreciated Grace's tact, but inwardly she was shaking. She had no idea what to say to her husband, who was now pouring himself a glass of iced tea. Her tongue felt like it was stuck to the roof of her mouth.

He trod across the boards, sat beside her, and took a sip of tea, the cubes rattling in his glass.

"Davis, I—" she managed to say, forcing the words past dry lips.

Davis put up a hand. "You don't have to say anything right now if you're not ready. I'm sure being unexpectedly here in your old hometown, for whatever reason, is hard enough." He set down the tea and shifted in his seat to face her. "I love you, Anne. I'll wait for you to tell me your story in your own time." His lips twisted in an expression of pain. "But don't take too long about it, okay?"

He loved her. She knew it, the same way she knew she loved him. But was she ready to put that love to the test?

12

Grace

Grace crossed the grass lawn, glancing over her shoulder a couple of times at the troubled couple on the porch. By the time she reached the dock, Spencer was tying his boat alongside the small watercraft the inn owned.

"Hey, Spencer. What brings you here?" Grace stepped onto the boards, greeting him with a smile. She'd been out a couple of times in his boat, a well-kept center-console model he used for fishing and picnics.

He unfolded his tall, lanky body and stood, giving Grace his easy smile. "Hey, Grace. Sorry to pop in on you this way, last minute. I was headed to town for dinner when I remembered the water luminaria launch tonight. I thought you might like to go." His expression sobered. "But you're probably busy with the inn. I should have thought of that."

"Luminaria launch?" Grace thought she'd heard something about it in the chamber meetings. But there had been so many activities planned, she couldn't remember them all.

"Yes, those little candles in paper bags? You can buy one as a fundraiser for the homeless shelter," Spencer said. "They're releasing them into the water to float across the lake at sunset."

That sounded magical. Grace glanced back at the inn, then down at her clothing. "Let me check with Charlotte to see if she minds. We have our usual wine and cheese hour tonight. And I need to change." One of the nice things about working with her sister was the flexibility it provided if one of them was sick or had to be somewhere. Of course, this didn't fit in the category of "have to," but it would be fun.

Spencer climbed aboard and settled back in his captain's chair, crossing his arms. "Take your time. I'll wait." He glanced up at the deep-blue sky. "I don't mind a bit. It's a gorgeous day to be outside."

"It sure is." Promising not to take long, Grace made the return trip across the lawn to the inn. As she hurried along, her mind turned over outfit possibilities, just in case she did go. Jeans, of course, and a jacket, since the air would get chilly later, especially on the water.

In the kitchen, Winnie was helping Charlotte prepare the platters of cold appetizers.

"Winnie," Grace exclaimed. "What are you doing here?" When she'd walked outside a few minutes ago, her aunt had been nowhere in sight.

"I thought I'd help out tonight," Winnie said. She picked up another carrot and began slicing it into sticks for dipping. On the platters beside her were heaps of celery sticks, mushroom caps, and broccoli florets.

Grace shook her head. Her aunt had the uncanny knack of showing up whenever they needed her. "That's great." She paused. "Especially since Spencer just asked me to go to the luminaria launch. He's waiting in his boat at the dock for an answer." She cringed in guilt. "Although I really shouldn't leave all the work to you two."

"Don't worry about it." Winnie winked. "You're off the hook."

Charlotte rolled a slice of ham with deft fingers and added it to a tray. "I suppose we can give you the night off," she said with a grin. "Have fun."

After thanking them, Grace headed for her room, where she flipped through her closet and drawers for the right clothing. She settled on a floaty, floral top that was perfect with her favorite pair of faded jeans. She slipped into a pair of moccasins and grabbed a denim jacket that looked cute and was just warm enough on a May night. After adding dangling glass bead earrings, a spritz of perfume, and a light application of makeup, she was ready.

After a quick goodbye to Charlotte and Winnie, she crossed the grass to the dock. True to his word, Spencer appeared perfectly relaxed in his seat, but when he saw her he jumped. "I take it you're coming with me."

"I am. Winnie happened to show up, so it all worked out." Grace clasped the warm, firm hand he held out to help her on board. She stepped into the craft, which rocked slightly and made her laugh.

"Easy, now." Spencer helped her to the other seat then untied the lines. He joined her at the console and soon the boat was cutting through the placid water, leaving a rippling wake.

"What a beautiful evening," Grace said. Arching sky and lake formed a bowl of blue, trimmed by the green trees and an eclectic variety of houses lining the shore.

Straight ahead lay their destination, the picturesque town of Magnolia Harbor set on its rolling hills. The harbor teemed with life, with boats humming in and out of the marina and throngs of people milling around the lakeside park.

Hands on the wheel, Spencer gazed around at the view. "I love it here." He pointed to a pair of waterfowl flapping overhead. "I feel like those ducks, as if I've come home to roost." Before retiring from the FBI and moving to Magnolia Harbor the year before, Spencer's work had taken him around the world.

"I feel the same way," Grace said. She and Charlotte had been born and raised in Magnolia Harbor, but Grace had lived in Charleston for almost twenty years. Buying the inn had been a return to her roots. Maybe her son, Jake, in his twenties and a computer programmer in Raleigh, North Carolina, would move back home at some point.

She could only hope. Right now she was glad he was enjoying his independence and career.

Spencer pointed the boat toward the public docks, where there were free tie-ups. "It's kind of fun going to town this way," he said. "In the height of tourist season, it's actually faster."

"I believe that," Grace said. Like most destination towns, Magnolia Harbor had wide swings in activity. Many businesses benefited from the visitors—as did the inn—but more than one owner heaved a sigh of relief when things slowed down briefly.

As they drew closer to shore, Grace heard lively notes from the band playing on stage. Noise and music from games and kiddy rides added to the commotion. Spencer lifted his nose to give an exaggerated inhale. "You smell that? Barbecue."

As Charlotte had once told Grace over a plate of ribs, the simple, delectable meal called barbecue was not only a signature Southern dish, it had almost as many recipes as cooks. According to her sister, controversies raged over sauce, tools, and techniques. Dry or wet rub. Pit or spit. Type of meat. Choice of sides.

Grace didn't debate it, she just ate it. An idea flitted through her mind . . . but it was lost to the distraction of Spencer finding a space to tie up, then the two of them leaving the boat and making their way toward the activities.

"Are you hungry?" Spencer asked. "Or would you like to look around first?"

"Let's do that and really build up an appetite," Grace said. She was eager to check out the booths. The listing of attendees had included some intriguing artists and craftspeople. Food products too. She liked to buy locally made goods to serve at the inn.

They poked along, looking at sweetgrass baskets and handcrafted leather goods, silver jewelry and dishes fired from local clay. All the vendors were from the surrounding area.

"I want everything," Grace said. "What beautiful work. Yummy too." She'd grabbed a card from a relish maker. The pepper relish would be perfect to go with a wine and cheese hour at the inn.

"I'm very impressed with the quality," Spencer said. He'd been as interested as Grace in examining the artisans' efforts, even pausing to ask questions. He'd bought a new leather wallet and made a deposit on a gorgeous red double-armed urn. He'd said he planned to display the lovely piece in his entryway.

As for Grace, she couldn't resist a pair of earrings made with tiny shells and freshwater pearls. She buttoned the little bag securely in her jacket pocket. "I'm hungry now," she said, smiling at Spencer. "Lead on."

He guided her through the tightly pressed crowds, winding a path toward the barbecue booth near the stage. They were passing a beanbag-tossing game when a loud voice caught Grace's ear. She glanced over and what she saw made her steps falter.

Troy stood nearby, hands on his hips and his face beet red with anger. "I don't like you hanging around with him. I thought you were dating me." He jabbed a finger toward his own broad chest, which was puffed up with outrage.

Presley narrowed her eyes, her hands fisted as she leaned close. "We've been dating all of a month. And if I want to spend time with an old friend, what business is it of yours?"

Grace knew she was being nosy by eavesdropping but she couldn't make her feet move. She put her hand inside her pocket and wrapped her fingers around her cell phone, just in case things got out of control. Spencer watched the situation, poised to spring into action, his former profession still evident in his stance.

"Old friend?" Troy scoffed. "Right. Keep telling yourself that." He pivoted on his heel and strode away, leaving Presley staring after him in dismay. Then she shook her own head and went in the opposite direction, thankfully not noticing Grace.

"What was that all about?" Spencer asked. "Friends of yours?"

Grace leaned close so he could hear her over the shouts of a nearby barker. "Not exactly. One of my current guests used to date Presley. She's a nurse at the hospital. Looks to me like the main impediment just went goodbye."

"The young man?" Spencer's nod was wise. "Yes, he blew it by pitching a fit."

"Hard to say. It may have been premature—or just the nudge Presley needs." Grace was sympathetic to Curt's quest but wise enough to know the feelings had to be mutual. Hopefully they were. She adored happy endings.

At the barbecue booth, they studied the chalkboard menu. "I'll have baby back ribs on a bun and coleslaw," Grace said. "With extra sauce."

"Beef brisket for me," Spencer said. "And potato salad." He glanced at Grace. "Want to split a bowl of collards?"

"Sure." She found a place at a picnic table while Spencer went to place the order. People-watching was fun at these events, which brought a mix of young and old, families and singles. She spotted Anne and Davis strolling arm in arm, poor Anne still looking strained and unhappy.

Grace lifted a quick prayer for the couple. When she and Charlotte had first talked about running an inn, she'd wanted it to be more than beds to sleep in for a night. She'd hoped that time spent there would restore and refresh, even heal. She had the distinct feeling that, like many other guests she'd hosted, Anne and Davis desperately needed a time of renewal.

"Hey, Grace. How are you?" Without invitation, Nancy Higgins, an older woman who was known for her pointed opinions, most of them unpleasant, perched on the bench across from her.

"I'm fine, thanks. We're really busy." Grace always made sure to cast everything she told Nancy in a positive light. "How are you?"

Nancy made a face and flapped a hand, her bracelets jingling. "Can't complain." She scanned the crowd with pursed lips. "Sure was surprised to see an old friend here at the festival." She swung around, her eyes voracious. "I think she's staying with you."

Grace didn't want to pursue this gossip about one of her guests and was about to say so when Spencer came into view, carrying a tray. "I'm sorry, Nancy," she said, happy for the excuse to discontinue the conversation. "But we're about to eat. Catch up later?"

Nancy grunted as she pushed herself to her feet. "I'd best be going anyway. Buford is waiting for me." She cocked her head at Spencer, raking him from head to toe, obviously waiting for an introduction.

"Oh, Nancy, this is Spencer Lewis. He bought Blossom Hill Farm. Spencer, Nancy Higgins. Nancy is really active in the community." Grace didn't elaborate.

Spencer put the tray down and shook Nancy's hand. Then, thankfully, the matron bustled off to snag a new victim.

As they dug into their delicious dinner, Grace couldn't help but wonder who Nancy was referring to. None of her present guests had mentioned having any previous connection in Magnolia Harbor, except Curt. And Nancy had said, "she." Not that it was any of her business. She certainly didn't pry, preferring to wait for people to confide in her if they felt like doing so.

After eating, they wandered around a little more while listening to a folk singer, then purchased luminaria for the launch. This took place on the longest dock, near where a stream emptying into the lake provided an outgoing current. Along with Spencer and Grace, dozens of people were lined up waiting for the signal to set their lanterns in the water.

"What's going to happen to these once the candles go out?" Grace wondered. The square lantern was made of paper, which might dissolve in time, but she couldn't imagine having hundreds littering the lakeshore. The candles were battery-operated tea lights and those shouldn't be allowed to stay in the lake.

Spencer pointed to boats waiting offshore. "Volunteers are going to clean them up. See the big nets?" Several people were holding fishing nets on long poles. Inside the boats were tall trash bins.

"All right, everyone. We're about ready to begin." The crowd turned to the speaker, and Grace recognized Laura Greenlaw, mother of three. She saw the children standing near a tall man with glasses, no doubt their father. Tonight they were wearing cute playclothes instead of the strawberry costumes.

"Thanks for coming out tonight," Laura continued. "As you know this benefit is for our local homeless outreach. The funding will go to provide beds, food, and other services to these most needy of our citizens." She paused, blinking, and Grace sensed this outreach meant something personal to the young woman.

Laura cleared her throat. "When I give the signal, turn on your candles," she said, "then send them out into the water. As with all lights, they symbolize hope, help, and hospitality. They beckon us home." She motioned. "Glen, want to lead us in prayer?"

Glen Abrams, pastor of Fellowship Christian Church, stepped forward, his white Einstein hair blowing in the gentle breeze. Behind him, the sun lowered to the horizon, etching the hills with gold. "Let us pray."

After the solemn moment, Laura gave the signal. Everyone excitedly turned on the tiny lights and set the candles afloat. Grace pushed the switch on hers and set it back in the bag. Then she kneeled down and placed the bag in the water. Spencer did the same.

The candles were gradually pulled out into the lake by the currents, creating an enchanting sight. Tiny bobbing lights shone against the dark water, some grouped together while others strayed off on their own.

"Are you ready to head out?" Spencer asked after they watched for a while. Gradually the crowd had dispersed, going back to the festival area or heading for home.

Grace realized the air had gotten chilly. "I am." As they walked to his boat, she said, "This was fun. Thanks for asking me."

"Any time." He helped her onto the boat then followed, jumping nimbly onto the deck. Once she was settled, he started the engine and left the dock, circling out around the lanterns.

A moon was rising and the reflection it cast touched the group of lanterns, making them look like drops of moonlight rippling on the gentle waves. Spencer slowed the boat, allowing them time to revel in the glorious sight.

Grace absorbed the beauty of the night, committing it to memory. She glanced over at Spencer, who seemed equally enthralled.

A surge of gratitude filled her heart. The best experiences were even more special when shared with a friend.

Anne

Anne studied the attractive, lively faces around the restaurant table, softened and made more youthful in the flickering candlelight. Davis was talking about investments while Roger and Melvin, his new friends from the country club, listened. Sheila and Beth, their wives, were chatting about their experiences while staying in Magnolia Harbor. The two couples knew each other from Atlanta and had traveled here for a getaway celebrating Roger's sixtieth birthday.

Out on the lake, floating lanterns bobbed and eddied. Anne leaned back in her chair and watched as the glowing lights traveled the currents, coming together then moving apart. Then moving back together. Sort of like the way she and Davis did.

She'd been relieved—a little—when Davis had offered to give her time to tell him the rest of her secrets. But she knew the reprieve was only temporary. For whatever reason, the past was rearing its ugly head and she was being forced to take a good look at it. Coming to Magnolia Harbor, having Nancy recognize her, even her encounter with Winnie earlier.

Anne had been waiting in the lobby for Davis to bring the car around when Winnie had said something quite odd. The other woman had been straightening brochures in the rack when she mumbled, "Sometimes you just need to forgive someone. It's the only way to move forward."

"Excuse me?" Anne wasn't sure if the other woman was actually speaking to her.

Winnie's hands had stilled. "I'm sorry. Did I say that aloud? I was thinking about something."

"No problem." Anne laughed it off. "I do that all the time myself." She'd heard the crunch of tires on the gravel and seen the headlights, so with a good night to Winnie, she'd gone out to the car.

But now Winnie's words keep echoing in her head. *Forgive someone.* There was only one person whom Anne had never forgiven. And it wasn't her mother-in-law. It was her own mother, who had let her down so terribly. But how could she? No, forgiveness wasn't possible in this situation.

Maybe she should have taken Davis up on his offer to cut the trip short and go home. But strangely enough, that hadn't been appealing. She couldn't run away from herself, so what would be the point of going back?

"I'm going to try and convince Roger to retire here," Sheila said. "Wouldn't it be wonderful living in a small town like this, Anne?"

Her question startled Anne, and lost in her thoughts the way she was, it took her a moment to comprehend the words. "I suppose it has its advantages," she finally said. "But surely Atlanta is a great place to live."

"Oh, it is." Sheila's wide smile revealed perfect teeth. She was a former beauty pageant winner, she'd managed to let Anne know. She tossed her blonde head, the hair falling back into place perfectly. "I love all the cultural activities. Roger and I are big supporters of the arts." She named several well-known institutions. "If you look at their donor list, there we are, every year. It's such an honor."

Judging by Sheila's falsely modest expression, Anne guessed their gifts were substantial. This woman would have made a perfect daughter-in-law for Cora. Instead Davis's mother had gotten Anne, a misfit. Not that Anne didn't enjoy music, art, and theater. But she didn't use them to advance her social position.

"I love being part of the arts community in the city," Beth gushed. "Did I tell you about the times we went backstage at the Georgia Music Hall of Fame Awards?"

Sheila's brow furrowed, the best it could with the paralyzing injections it'd clearly endured. That had been another topic of conversation, the women's relentless assault on the indignities of aging. "I think you did, Beth."

"Pish." Beth waved a dismissive hand then leaned forward across the table. "Anne hasn't heard about it." She proceeded to detail her encounters with famous musical performers, all of them flattering to her.

As the woman nattered on, Anne did her best to listen. But she couldn't help but wonder how many hours she'd endured with people destined to never be more than acquaintances. Not that she didn't like meeting new people and hearing their stories. She did. But most of the time *her* personality and experiences were safely hidden behind the socially acceptable shell of Anne Montgomery, wife of Davis, daughter-in-law of Cora, and mother of Austin.

A realization brought her up short. How could she reveal her most inner, sacred self to anyone when she was hiding it from those who really mattered? Namely, her family. And even herself.

For most visitors, Magnolia Harbor was surely a beautiful, relaxing place to visit. For Anne, it was proving to be a battleground. Within her own heart.

"That was fun, wasn't it?" Davis asked on the way back to the inn. "What great people. Roger invited us down to their Buckhead house." He chuckled. "Apparently there are a lot of nice courses around

Atlanta." The night out had succeeded in easing the tension between them, and Anne was grateful for that.

And what would Anne do in Buckhead? Go shopping or visit the dermatologist with the wives while hearing about their latest exploits and triumphs? She knew her thoughts were mean but she managed to shove them down with a big swallow. "Sheila and Beth are quite active in the arts community, bless their hearts." Her voice was as dry as a clay road in August.

"But?" Davis wasn't a pointed-pencil accountant for nothing. He could pick out a social falsity with lightning speed. The bigger ones he wasn't so attuned to, obviously. "You didn't like them?"

Anne sighed. How could she stop this conversation from sliding downhill like that clay road in a rainstorm? "They were fine. Really nice women, in fact. If you want to visit Roger and go golfing, I'm all for it." She injected a jovial note into her voice. "Just give me your credit card and set me loose in those department stores."

That distracted him, as she knew it would. "Well, Anne, I'm retired now so we're going to have to—"

"Be careful, I know." She patted his arm. "I was just joshing you. Those women sure can shop so they'll expect me to keep up, that's all." She shrugged as if it wasn't any big deal.

He fell silent, eyes focused on the road, teeth worrying his bottom lip. "I have an idea for tomorrow," he finally said. "Want to go out to the barrier islands? I thought we could snorkel and have a picnic on the beach."

A day away from Magnolia Harbor and her churning emotions sounded perfect. "I'd love to do that, Davis. You know how much I enjoy going to the beach." Living so far inland, they rarely had the opportunity.

"It's a plan, then. We'll get up early and mosey down to the coast." Davis signaled and slowed as they reached the entrance to the inn. He parked in the lot. "Don't get out." He came around and opened the door for Anne, a courtesy that he hadn't given her for ages. On impulse, she took his arm as they strolled to the building. He slowed to match his stride to hers, rather than bolting ahead as usual.

How long had it been since they'd acted like a couple in love? *Far too long*, Anne decided. "What a beautiful night," she said. The night air was soft and warm, carrying the scent of night-blooming jasmine. "I hate to go inside."

"Nothing says we have to," Davis said. "Remember, Grace said we had the run of the place." When they stepped onto the veranda, he guided her around the side to the back. Anne sat on a teak lounge chair and he settled on the one next to her. They both leaned back against thick cushions and studied the nighttime view of lake and sky.

Her husband sighed deeply. "This is what it's all about, isn't it, darling? You and me taking it easy and enjoying our time together. We've earned it."

Anne's heart clenched. He was right. All through the years of building the business, making sacrifices, enduring lean times, the promise of retirement had glimmered like an oasis. They were so fortunate to have made it this far. Some of their friends were already widowed, left to face their elderly years alone. They'd had a medical scare or two, of course. No one escaped those. But she and Davis were in pretty good shape, considering.

That was why it was critical she didn't blow it now. But would their marriage survive the truth?

Davis's hand fumbled for hers, the chairs close enough that they could hold hands comfortably. They chatted about this and that, nothing of importance. But despite how pleasant it was on the veranda, night insects buzzing, the moon rising over the lake, Anne's secrets sat on her chest like the proverbial elephant in the room.

Why couldn't she leave it alone? Obviously—and thankfully—he wasn't pressuring her for answers. Yet. Maybe he never would. Maybe he'd forget the whole thing, decide the past wasn't worth digging into—

"Anne." He squeezed her fingers. "I know I said I wouldn't push. And I'm not, honestly." He paused. "But don't you *trust* me?"

The anguish in his voice cut Anne's heart to ribbons. She'd been so wrapped up in her own thoughts and feelings she'd failed to consider what this was doing to him.

"Oh, Davis," she said, the words rushing out. "Of course I trust you, it's not that." She took a deep, shuddering breath. Words rose up in a snarled mass, crowding to her lips. *My mother . . . she was . . . you need to understand . . . I couldn't . . .*

The words in her mind were a jumble, incoherent.

How could she tell a man who was doted upon by his mother that her own had been cold and aloof? Oh, Anne had had all the physical blessings, but emotionally she'd been an orphan, never able to please her mother and meet her standards. Davis probably wouldn't believe her. And perhaps he'd think that Anne was flawed, undeserving of love—

The door opened behind them and a woman slipped outside.

Bridget O'Brien, that was her name. She was writing a book, Anne remembered. Bridget spotted them and took a step back. "Oh, I'm sorry. I didn't know you were out here." She turned to go back inside. "I'll leave you be."

Coward that she was, Anne greeted this interruption with a relief so intense it made her go limp. "That's all right," she said. "We're just sitting here." Davis squeezed her hand again and let go, settling back with a gentle sigh, so soft only Anne heard it, she was sure.

"Okay, if you're sure you don't mind." Bridget selected a rocker and began to propel the chair back and forth, gentle squeaks sounding from the wood. "What a night. I'm starting to really love the South."

Grace was the next to appear. "Anyone want cookies and milk? I'll bring out a tray."

"That sounds great, Grace," Anne said. "I was too full for dessert but I could eat a cookie now."

After the innkeeper popped back inside, Anne turned to Bridget. "Are you having good luck researching your book?"

Bridget rocked. "I am. Although I've kind of come to a dead end on one part of my project."

"Really? What's that?" Anne was merely being polite, but she wanted to fill the silence emanating from her husband.

"I'm trying to figure out how someone can track down a birth parent. It's not easy if the adoption was sealed."

Anne felt her spine straighten. Of all the subjects Bridget could have brought up, Anne hadn't expected that one. "I imagine it would be difficult," Anne said. Surely that was the point of sealed records. It was much simpler to pretend the biological parents didn't exist, right? An approach Anne thought was gravely flawed. "With no information, where would you begin?"

Air whooshed out of Bridget. "That's exactly the problem. My . . . character has barely anything to go on."

"Do people still do that? Give up kids for adoption?" Davis asked, his masculine voice startling in the quiet hush. "I really can't understand how someone can give up their own flesh and blood." If Davis had a fault, it was the blunt statements he sometimes made without regard to his audience. Anne tended to temporize, to shade her responses so as not to offend.

"I think they do it because they don't see another option," Bridget said. When Davis started to speak again, she held up a hand. "I believe they've come to the agonizing conclusion that it's better for the child."

Anne sent her husband a glare and he subsided with a grumble.

"I think you're right, Bridget," she said.

Bridget accepted her words with a grateful nod, and something about her expression made Anne wonder if the issue was personal. She seemed too invested for someone just writing a book about the topic.

The door opened again and Grace and Charlotte emerged onto the porch, both holding snacks. If they sensed the tense atmosphere, they didn't give any sign.

"Here we are," Grace said, setting down a tray. "Fresh out of the oven." She poured three glasses of milk and, after the beverages were served, she sat on a nearby sofa.

"These are from my new recipe for strawberry cream cheese cookies," Charlotte said. She passed the plate around and they each took one of the big, soft circles.

Davis munched on the treat, his good humor seeming to be restored. "This reminds me of the nightly snacks my mama prepared for me. Homemade cookies and milk, before bedtime."

"She still would, if I let her," Anne said, her tone tart. She had been joking, but even though it didn't really sound that way, the others laughed gently.

Charlotte took the rocker next to Bridget. "I wanted to ask you all something. I'm entering a strawberry entrée contest and I'd like to have you test some samples tomorrow night at dinner."

Anne, thankful for the change of subject, said, "I'll taste test, no problem."

"Me too," Davis said.

"I'm in," Bridget said. "It sounds fun, especially if you win. We'll make sure we go to the contest and root for you."

"It's not going to be easy," Charlotte said with a laugh. "There are some excellent chefs in Magnolia Harbor."

"The dinner we had tonight was very good, I have to admit," Anne said. "We ate at The Tidewater."

Charlotte groaned and Grace leaped to explain. "The head chef there is the man to beat. At least in Charlotte's eyes."

"Well, I wouldn't say . . . yeah, I guess I would." Charlotte nodded. "What did you have, Anne?"

"The strawberry-infused scallops. Melt-in-your-mouth good, but of course they were really fresh." Anne winced, hoping she wasn't hurting Charlotte's feelings somehow.

"I had those too." Charlotte sounded glum. "They're fantastic."

Grace made a sound. "Charlotte, I had a thought while I was at the festival tonight with Spencer."

Her sister's brows rose. "Oh? And what was that thought?" Her tone was teasing.

Grace rolled her eyes. "Spencer and I had barbecue. I think some kind of strawberry-inspired barbecue dish would be perfect."

"It would," Anne said. "The festival is casual, right? So the food should be too."

Charlotte appeared skeptical. "You think? Because if there's one thing Dean isn't, it's casual about cooking. He's always raising the bar."

"There's nothing more Southern than barbecue," Davis said. "I say go for it."

Bridget chimed in with her agreement. "It's worth a try. And we'll be honest about what we think. Right, Anne?"

"Of course," Anne said. "Though I'm sure we'll have nothing but praise. You're a fabulous chef."

Charlotte brushed off the compliment, but Anne could tell she was pleased. She changed the subject, asking the guests their impressions of Strawberry Fest so far.

After another cookie, Davis turned to Anne. "Ready to go up?" She nodded yes, so he added, "We've got an early morning tomorrow."

That gave rise to questions about their plans and, after getting some great advice, Anne and Davis went up to their room.

"I'm looking forward to the beach," Anne said as Davis unlocked the door. She held her breath, hoping that he wouldn't return to the topic of her past.

"Me too." He pushed the door open to let her enter first. "How long has it been, Annie?" That was one of his pet names for her, and when she heard it, the anxiety drained out of her like a balloon losing air.

Maybe it was only a delay, but for tonight, she and her secrets were safe.

14

Charlotte

Grace's suggestion about the contest entry niggled in Charlotte's mind all night, to the point where she even dreamed about barbecuing giant strawberries on a grill. The oversize fruit didn't want to cooperate and, in the way of dreams, even came alive and ran away. So she told the judges she was dropping out of the contest, only to watch in frustration while Dean won first place.

When the alarm shrilled, she was actually happy to wake up for once. The downside of serving breakfast at the inn was getting up at five o'clock, but if that was her only complaint, she was a lucky woman. After jumping in the shower, she got dressed, then strolled through the misty, fragrant morning the short distance from her cottage to the inn.

Every day the gardens looked slightly different, due to the changeable weather and time of year. This morning the magnolia trees were laden, the blossoms starlike against the glossy foliage. Birds chirped and darted, flying down to the grass for worms and insects.

An odd shape came trundling around a holly bush, and Charlotte's heart gave a painful lurch. A giant strawberry with huge eyes and a grinning mouth stopped and stared at her. For a disorienting moment she wondered if she was still asleep. She'd dreamed about waking up before, an odd dream within a dream. She pinched her forearm. *Ouch.* No, she was awake all right.

The fruit started marching toward her, tiny green arms waving. Charlotte hesitated, fighting the urge to run. A muffled voice shouted something but she couldn't make out the words.

The costume contest. This had to be another stray entrant, one who was out and about far too early. Charlotte wished she'd at least had a cup of coffee before she had to deal with this. As for the contestant, he or she must be roasting inside that thing, even in the cool morning temperatures.

The strawberry stopped a few feet away. "Can you judge my costume?" a male voice said, still muffled but clearer. A green hand swiped at the fruit's side and pulled out a scorecard from somewhere.

Charlotte winced. "I'm sorry, but we aren't doing that here. The newspaper made a mistake."

The green hands tucked the scorecard away then went up and pulled at the costume. The top half popped off to reveal a young man with tousled hair. "Seriously?" he said. "I'm dying in this thing."

"I wouldn't lie to you," Charlotte said. "You've got one of the best costumes I've seen so far." She started walking toward the inn. "Would you like a cup of coffee and a muffin? I can do that much for you at least."

His grin shone with relief. "Thanks. I could really use a cup of coffee." He tripped along behind her, the head under his arm, and Charlotte had to smile at the picture they must present to anyone watching. *Chef leads giant strawberry to slaughter?*

When they reached the side door leading to the kitchen, she said, "If you go around to the back veranda, I'll bring you coffee."

"That way?" He pointed and, at her nod, kept going.

Charlotte was first to arrive in the kitchen. She put on an apron then puttered around, starting coffee and pulling out ingredients for muffins. Today she would make raspberry—not strawberry—streusel along with bacon and cheese omelets. Once the coffee was brewed, she set a mug on a tray along with carrot muffins from yesterday and carried it out to the veranda. Bridget was already there, seated next to the young man and chatting. She held her ever-present notebook and pen.

"Good morning. I would have brought you a cup had I known you were up so early," Charlotte said.

Bridget waved that off. "Thanks, but I'll come inside in a few. I'm going to take a stroll around the garden and enjoy the morning first." She smiled at the young man, who was devouring a muffin. "Are there any more like you lurking in the garden?"

"No, I'm last of my breed," he quipped. "Or should it be species?" The women laughed.

Grace soon appeared in the kitchen, diving in to help Charlotte with breakfast duties. Charlotte glanced at the clock. "I was hoping to dash to the farmers market once everything is under control."

"Go ahead." Grace made a shooing motion. "I'll make the omelets as people come down." Crispy bacon was waiting on one platter, grated cheese on another.

Charlotte pulled off her apron and hung it on a hook, grateful as always that she had Grace as her business partner. Between the two of them, and with Winnie's help, they managed to get everything done while still having time to pursue their own interests.

She grabbed a couple of cloth bags and hopped into her Camry sedan, then headed toward town. The farmers market was located in a pavilion near the railroad tracks. Decades ago, the open-air building had been a holding spot for produce ready to be shipped out or brought in from elsewhere. Now, vendors set up tables inside and shoppers wandered through from one end to the other.

Charlotte paused near the entrance, her attention caught by the colorful and delicious array. Baskets of bright green beans and pea pods. Ruby-red globes of beets and radishes. Early corn. Seafood too—shrimp on ice, whole fish, and crabs.

She spotted plump, fresh chickens—maybe she *should* try barbecuing breasts and thighs with a tangy strawberry sauce. She began to push her way into the throng.

A hand clutched her upper arm, stopping her progress. "Charlotte. How's it going?" Dean's brown eyes smiled down at her. Wearing a crisp T-shirt and faded jeans, he looked wide awake, even this early in the day.

Deciding to focus on his question, she waved her list. "Great. Just picking up a few things for the inn." Nothing would induce her to mention the swiftly approaching contest. She'd let him think she was ready to compete, not scrambling to create a winning entry.

He folded his arms across his chest. "All set for the contest?"

How did he do that? "Um, yes, of course. Got a great recipe, but of course it's a secret." Giving a totally fake chuckle, she tore her eyes away and glanced around the pavilion, hoping she looked like someone with shopping on her mind. "Is the honey vendor here?" *Oops*. She hadn't meant to mention that to him. She liked using honey in her homemade barbecue sauce.

"He was here last week. Want to go look?" Dean took her elbow and guided her into the stream of customers. "Let's go through together. It will be fun."

Great. Unless she forced herself to be incredibly rude, she was stuck with Dean's company while she shopped—and sought inspiration—for her supposedly top-secret recipe. One she hadn't invented yet.

First he bought her a cup of coffee, made right there from freshly roasted and ground beans. "I love the aroma of roasting beans," Charlotte said. "Yum."

"I've toyed with the idea of roasting my own," Dean said. He took a contemplative sip. "I'd call the company Tidewater Roasters."

"Great idea," Charlotte said. "You could sell the beans to guests to take home." Holding their cups, they sidled through the crowd. "I want to get some of those green beans and peas." Her chef's palate longed for those first delectable bites of the season's bounty.

Dean waited while she selected and purchased the vegetables. Then it was on to taste goat cheese from a new vendor. They bantered back and forth about the best flavors, Dean favoring the cracked pepper and Charlotte the basil. Charlotte bought a couple of tubs for the afternoon social and Dean placed a bulk order for his restaurant.

"I'm going to use it on a tomato tart," he said. He described the dish so well Charlotte could practically see and taste it.

She felt a wistful tug toward the past. When she was a chef in Charleston, she had created new menus weekly, if not daily. It had been an ongoing challenge to source and incorporate the best of what was available locally and in season.

But she didn't miss the pressure or the personalities, she reminded herself. She was captain—well, cocaptain—of her own ship here and it was fantastic. Designing the occasional dish, like the barbecued chicken grilled in savory, sweet, spicy strawberry sauce that was taking shape in her mind, added the perfect dash of challenge to her life. Her mind lit up as the ingredients she needed scrolled through her mind in a sudden burst of inspiration. And she'd use chicken wing drumettes, tiny bites of mouthwatering goodness that came with their own bone handles, instead of larger breasts or tenders.

Charlotte smiled at Dean, confident in her idea and not caring if he guessed what she was doing. "Honey vendor next? I need some for a recipe."

Bridget

"What are you up to today?" Bridget asked Curt. They were seated in the dining room enjoying breakfast. Curt had entered the room whistling, and somehow he was managing to eat breakfast while smiling the entire time.

The young doctor's grin grew even larger. "Presley and I are taking a day trip down to Charleston."

Grace, who was carrying a fresh carafe of coffee into the room, overheard. "That's super, Curt. If you need any recommendations, I can help." She switched out the coffeepots. "I lived in Charleston for twenty years." She lingered in the dining room, clearing up empty dishes and giving him suggestions for sightseeing and restaurants. The Montgomerys had just left on their way to the ocean.

A wave of forlorn longing washed over Bridget. All these happy couples going out for the day. And while she didn't envy them exactly, she missed her own love, Sean.

She sternly brought her mind back to her mission. She was here for a purpose, one that was more important than having fun. And when she went home, she'd make a date with her darling husband. They needed to do that more often, and now that Molly was getting older, they really didn't have any excuses. Their daughter didn't require a babysitter anymore.

It was all too easy to stay busy with the "have-tos" and neglect what really mattered, she reflected. Spending time with family and friends should be at the top of her list, not last.

Once Curt and Grace finished their discussion, Bridget asked, "Grace, do you know where I can get something notarized?" She'd learned during her perusal of the adoption registry that she should fill out an affidavit and have it notarized. Then the state could release nonidentifying information about her family and, if there was mutual consent, the identity of her birth parents. At the very least, she might learn something about her medical history.

"You can go to my bank," Grace said. "Mention my name and that you're a guest."

Bridget wrote down the name of the bank, which was located downtown. She'd get the document notarized, then go back to the library to do some more research. Her heart skipped a beat when she recalled the woman in the portrait wearing the locket so like hers. She'd start with the Jackson family.

But before she ventured out, she decided, she needed to get some writing done. The deadline clock for Annabelle's story had started to tick, and she needed to produce at least a thousand words, about four pages, every day. Starting now.

After breakfast, Bridget filled a mug with coffee and went up to her room. She was enjoying her little lair, the privacy and comfort at the top of the house making it a perfect writing spot. The morning air was still cool, so she opened the veranda doors before settling in at the small writing desk. Had someone like Annabelle sat at this desk? She would have used a quill or a fountain pen, if so.

How much longer would it take to write a book by hand, as writers of old had done? How tedious it would be to edit and then write a clean copy. Bridget shook her head, grateful for the irony of modern technology that allowed her to efficiently write novels set in the past.

She flipped open her laptop and watched as the screen gradually came to life. The first step was to open a document file. Next she set up the heading and format.

Then she stared at the blank screen.

Beginnings. They were the worst. Well, next to middles, when a writer's energy and ideas often sagged. Endings were good. No, they were great, the words, "The End" perhaps the most satisfying in a writer's vocabulary.

Bridget typed a few sentences, deleted them, and tried again. No, that still wasn't right. Maybe moving around would help. She stood up and went out on the veranda.

Sean. She could send him a text to check in. He'd get back to her during his break. Fully aware she was stalling, Bridget sent him a cute note with lots of hearts and kisses. Then she scrolled through pictures, smiling at Molly's antics in many. They always had so much fun on outings to the aquarium and the science and fine arts museums in downtown Boston.

Okay. Enough. Bridget put the phone down and paced. A few words drifted into her mind.

Snapping her parasol open, Annabelle stepped off the veranda into a brilliant summer afternoon.

Bridget hurried into the room and sat at the keyboard, tapping in the opening line before she lost it. The words continued to come. Maybe they weren't perfect but they were a start.

Annabelle strolled along the azalea-lined path, grateful someone had invented such a flattering piece of froth to shield her face from sunlight. Freckles would ruin her chances to marry, her mother—

Bridget snorted, thankful that her freckles hadn't scared Sean off. That reminded her, Sean hadn't texted back. She frowned, one corner of her mind registering that fact while the words continued to flow. But maybe he'd had a meeting.

It didn't take long to reach her word count and she considered going on, but she sometimes found that was counterproductive. So she made a few notes for tomorrow's writing session, saved her document, and left the inn. She took the bus downtown again, not wanting to deal with traffic and parking. The little village was starting to feel familiar, and she studied the homes and businesses with the sense of checking on old friends. Was she rooted in this place? The wave of longing for connection she'd felt at breakfast returned, even stronger this time. She'd liked her suburban Boston town all right. It had been a fine place to grow up. But urban sprawl mushroomed every year, commercial development swallowing green space, old neighborhoods replaced by new.

Was her reaction due to subconscious, even inherited, memories or was it mere sentiment? As a writer she had the ability to immerse herself in new experiences, new places. The fact that she could imagine herself growing up in this beautiful place would help her create Annabelle's story.

She closed her eyes and inhaled, wanting to imprint the distinctively Southern scents of a warm early summer day. A woman of Annabelle's day wouldn't have had to inhale the odor of gasoline, but the sunbaked clay soil and varied flower scents would have been the same, and so would the hint of fresh water and fish from the lake.

In the heart of downtown, Bridget emerged from the shuttle, immediately spotting the bank building on the corner of Magnolia and Main. The historic brick three-story building was ornately trimmed with granite, giving it an aura of wealth and power.

Bridget pushed through tall doors into a large, cool lobby where three tellers stood behind a carved teller station. To the right was a desk placed near several potted trees.

The woman seated behind the desk stopped typing on her keyboard and smiled. "May I help you?" she asked in a thick Southern accent. *Nora Jean Parsons, Customer Service Manager*, a nameplate read.

"I hope so." Bridget slid into one of the padded chairs in front of the desk. "Grace Porter at Magnolia Harbor Inn said I could get something notarized here. I'm a guest of the inn."

"Miss Grace sent you?" She cocked her head, studying Bridget with bright blue eyes ringed with matching eyeliner. "Then yes, we'll be glad to assist you."

Bridget pulled out her driver's license and gave it to the representative. Then she signed the affidavit and pushed it across the glossy wood surface. She held her breath, wondering if the woman would read the document and perhaps even question her. But no, she was entirely professional as she embossed the form with her notary seal and filled in the blanks.

"Is there anything else I can do for you?" Nora Jean asked after she returned the affidavit.

"That's it, thank you." Bridget tucked the form into an envelope. She was going to drop it in the mail with overnight delivery. She'd also signed up with that online registry Presley had told her about. Was it too soon to hope for a match?

"Have a great day." Nora Jean's smile followed her out the doors to the sidewalk.

Bridget stopped by the post office to mail the letter, then continued on to the library. The route took her past the Jackson mansion and she stopped to stare at it for a minute. Was it possible that Olympia Jackson was her grandmother? A sensation of disbelief swept over her. It was like something out of a novel, the long-lost heiress discovering she was from a wealthy and prominent family.

But in this case, her inheritance now belonged to the town. All she had was her locket. But of course it wasn't about the money. It was about . . . finding the truth about herself.

At the library, Phyllis greeted her with a wave. "Back to do more research?" she asked. She picked up a book and scanned it for the older woman standing at the desk.

"I am," Bridget said, appreciating the fact that Phyllis remembered her. She moved up to the desk and stood beside the patron. "I'm looking into the history of the Jackson family. I'm going to use their house in my book." For Annabelle's love interest.

"There's a lot about the Jacksons in the local history section," Phyllis said. "They were one of the first families to settle in Magnolia Harbor."

Bridget's heart skipped a beat. She'd always envied Sean's big family, with their long history in the Boston area and wealth of stories. To think that she might be able to learn about her ancestors was a thrill. If the Jacksons *were* her ancestors.

"That's an unusual locket you're wearing," the library patron said, cocking her head like an inquisitive bird. She was tiny and frail, with pointed features and close-cropped curls that furthered the impression.

Bridget held out the locket for her inspection. "It is. I inherited it from my mother."

The woman gazed at the locket then gave Bridget a sharp glance. "Would you like to come by my house tomorrow? I know a lot about the town's history."

"That's an understatement," Phyllis said. "Julep was president of the historical society for more years than I can count."

Julep scoffed. "I finally had to resign so someone else would take the reins."

With that endorsement, Bridget felt comfortable saying yes to the invitation. "I'd love to have tea with you. I'm staying in Magnolia Harbor a few more days."

"How about tomorrow?" Julep said. "Three o'clock, my house. I live on Lake Haven Road, about half a mile from the inn." She gave the address.

"That would be perfect," Bridget said. "I'll see you then." As she walked toward the research room, she replayed Julep's reaction to the locket in her mind. She had the distinct feeling that the historian had recognized it. Another sign that she was on the right track.

Bridget spent some time browsing the history shelves, finding a few tomes that detailed the settlement and growth of Magnolia Harbor. The Jacksons were mentioned frequently, but she didn't learn much more than what the docent had told her. They'd been prominent business owners and active in civic and church affairs also. She did learn that the male names tended to start with H: Heywood, Harrison, Harlon, and Halbert.

After putting the books back, she selected several boxes of microfilm. First she checked for Olympia Jackson's obituary. She'd died ten years ago, Becky Thomas had said. After scrolling through the entire year, she found it in December.

Bridget sighed. Wasn't that always the way? The obituary was brief, and to her disappointment, didn't list any offspring. There was a mention of Holland J. Jackson, Olympia's husband. He died in 1965.

Becky wasn't sure about any children or other family members, either.

Her hand went to her locket. Had she reached a dead end?

But she had a feeling her meeting tomorrow with Julep would reveal . . . something. She only hoped it would be something that wasn't better left buried.

16

Anne

"Isn't this great?" Davis raised his voice to be heard above the boat engine. They were on the early ferry to Daufuskie Island, a barrier island off the coast. He and Anne were standing at the bow rail, allowing the sea breeze to whip through their hair. The ocean was blue under a matching sky, the glistening waves topped with whitecaps.

Her husband's grin made Anne smile in response, and she felt her spirits lift. Leaving the mainland to head out into open water felt like shedding heavy baggage. Her problems were back on shore. Out here she was free. *They* were free.

Anne took her husband's hand and stood close, allowing his body to shelter her from the wind. There were other passengers riding the ferry but they were seated behind them. As she and Davis watched the island approach, it was as if they were alone in the world.

Well, almost. A large white sailboat cruised by, heeled over so the sail could catch the wind. The people on board waved. Anne waved back, enjoying the camaraderie of strangers on the sea.

Next a school of dolphins appeared, cavorting in the water to the delight of the onlookers.

"We should do this more often," she said into Davis's ear. Every time they traveled to the coast, she remembered how much she loved it. Austin had too, as a child. He'd play all day in the sand, shouting in joy as he dashed in and out of the water. By the end of the day he would be sunburned and covered in sand, his blond hair bleached almost white.

But he'd be happy and content, asleep before he finished his dinner.

Lake Haven was fun, too, she remembered. When she was young, she'd been allowed to roam through town with her friends. They'd go swimming most of the day, maybe mess around in boats, or ride their bicycles around the lake. Back then, fifty years ago, people didn't worry so much about children's safety. Besides, all the adults in town kept an eye on the kids. Anne and her friends knew that help—or a cold glass of lemonade—was only a word away.

But that long-gone world was harsher in some respects, the rules more rigid. Just look at her mother—Anne tore her thoughts back to the present. The ferry was slowing now, the captain cutting the engine as they approached the wharf. Water glided along the bow with a gurgle, and seagulls began to circle overhead with loud cries.

The island itself was a huddle of trees rimmed with golden sand. A humid haze lay over the land, further softening the view. This was a gentle shore, not the rockbound, dramatic coastline found in New England.

After the ferry was tied up, they disembarked and strolled along the lengthy wharf with the other passengers. "Where to?" Anne asked, shifting her tote to a more comfortable position on her shoulder. She'd packed a swimsuit, towel, sunscreen, book, camera, and more for their day trip.

Davis guided her forward with a hand on her lower back. "We're renting golf carts to tour the island. I thought we'd pick up lunch and go out to one of the lighthouses. Then after we sunbathe and eat, we can circle back and visit the historic district."

She couldn't have planned it better herself, and said so, punctuating her remark with a kiss on his cheek. While Davis handled the golf cart rental, Anne put her swimsuit on under her clothes in the restroom, just in case there wasn't a changing spot. Then she poked around the gift shop. She found a couple of things she wanted to pick up, but decided to wait until later. No sense carting gift bags around all day.

Davis soon pulled up in front with the cart so Anne hurried out to join in. She stowed her tote bag behind the seat and climbed in. "At least I know you're good at driving these," she said as they started off.

He threw her a smile. "That's right. So sit back, relax, and enjoy the tour." He foraged on the floor then handed her a map. "You can navigate."

Anne unfolded the map of the island. "Where to?"

"First I thought we'd stop and get lunch to go. Grace recommended a place."

Grace had also suggested Daufuskie Island, and so far Anne agreed it had been a great choice for a day trip. The vibe was relaxed and friendly. There were people around but it wasn't crowded, like some of the more popular destinations.

After finding the restaurant, which looked like a shack but put out great food, they bought shrimp salad sandwiches on homemade rolls, chips, bottles of iced tea, and a bag of ice. The sandwiches and tea went with the ice into the cooler they'd brought along.

"Want to check out Bloody Point Lighthouse?" Davis asked. "There's an island museum. Then we can go to the beach nearby."

Davis knew Anne loved museums. "That sounds perfect." She scanned the map for the lighthouse, which was clearly marked. It was located at the bottom of the five-mile-long island. "Take the next right and head south."

The golf cart zipped along a road shaded by moss-draped oaks. Here and there, historic bungalows were set under trees or in fields. Anne recognized some of these as examples of Gullah architecture, an African-based culture with a rich history on the Sea Islands.

Anne's thoughts drifted back to when she and Davis had met. After fleeing Magnolia Harbor, she had been a heartbroken, depressed mess. Before everything had gone wrong, making the first mistake that led to a cascade of others, she'd planned to attend Chapel Hill, a branch of the University of North Carolina. She moved to the nearby city of Durham, and without access to her family's resources, she entered college as a work-study student.

The day she'd met her husband Anne was working behind the counter in the cafeteria, hair in a net, no makeup, and stoically enduring snobby students who regarded all service workers beneath their notice or courtesy.

"Whoops." Notorious frat boy Sterling Jackson Davenport III dropped his loaded tray onto the floor with a crash. Chili, peas, cornbread, and chocolate mousse went everywhere, splattering the counter front and freckling the bare legs of the coed next to him. She screamed and ran for napkins to wipe her legs.

"You gonna clean that up, Davenport?" another student asked. This was Davis, although she didn't know his name yet. The students nearby and Anne and her coworkers waited to hear Sterling's answer.

Sterling ran a hand through thick blond hair and laughed. "Nah, man. That's for the help to take care of." He turned to his buddies. "Let's get out of here."

But Davis lingered, shaking his head when Sterling asked, "Coming, man?"

"Clean that up, Anne," her boss, a senior student, barked. Anne was the newest hire so she was the one who got all the nasty jobs. The fact that she'd turned him down for a date might or might not have had something to do with it too.

She grabbed a mop and bucket from the back, along with a pile of rags, resigned to the chore. To her surprise, Davis helped, seemingly heedless of the damage to his neatly pressed jeans. While crouched down cleaning up tomato sauce goo, he said, "What's a nice girl like you doing in a place like this?"

His corny comment broke the ice and by the time everything

was sparkling clean, he'd asked her to go with him to a rock concert. Concerts were big in those days, the late 1970s.

Anne smiled at the memory. Protective and kind, that was her Davis. She ran a hand down his bare forearm, earning a smile.

"Whatcha thinking about, Annie?" he asked.

"How we met in the cafeteria. And how nice of you it was to help me clean up that mess." Later she'd learned that Sterling and Davis were in the same fraternity. Sterling's reaction upon seeing Anne with Davis was to comment that she "cleaned up okay." Davis had almost punched him. After that Sterling stayed out of their way. He was even courteous in the cafeteria.

Davis chuckled. "I haven't thought about those good old boys forever." After a moment, he added, "Sterling had a heart attack last year and passed. I read about it in the alumni magazine."

Despite the fact she hadn't liked Sterling, Anne felt a pang. How meaningless all the strife and turmoil was in the end. Life was too short to neglect the important things.

Like those you cared about. And the truth. Certainty mingled with trepidation stirred in Anne's chest. She needed to tell Davis everything and do it soon.

But then her defenses immediately reared up. If only she could be certain that he would still love her. What if she lost him? Despite the day's heat, a bleak, cold feeling swept over Anne. In one part of her brain she knew this sensation was only a memory of her mother's rejection. But at the emotional, gut level, she was afraid to take the risk.

He hadn't pressed her for answers about her past, so why bring it up, a voice whispered. *Enjoy the day. Think of poor Sterling, who was the same age as Davis. You never know how many days you'll be allotted.*

Davis slowed at an intersection. "Which way?"

Anne consulted the map. "Left. That should take us straight there."

At the museum, located in the old lighthouse keeper's cottage, Anne and Davis learned the storied history of the island. It began in prehistoric times with the Muskogean Indians. Next, Spanish settlers brought Iberian horses, descendants of which remained on the island. Later, plantations grew Sea Island Cotton, and after the Civil War, the oyster trade flourished. And as she'd heard, the fascinating Gullah culture with its art, food, and music was still deeply entrenched on the island.

One of Anne's great-grandmothers hailed from the Sea Islands, and she told Davis that. The revelation was the tiniest of baby steps, but it was a start.

"That was interesting," Davis said as they exited the museum. "Especially hearing about your great-grandmother. But I'm ready for lunch on the beach."

Anne's belly rumbled. "Me too." As they set off on the cart again, she lifted her face to the breeze. It was a perfect beach day, sunny but not too hot. Breezy enough to keep the insects at bay.

The beach was three miles long, according to the map, and the couple easily found a private spot. Davis had brought an umbrella and he set that up while Anne laid out a blanket. After stripping down to her swimsuit, she anointed her too-pale skin with liberal amounts of sunscreen.

"Can you do my shoulders?" Davis took off his polo shirt and presented his back to Anne. He tanned easily and was already brown from the first swims of the season at the club.

"You're pretty hot for an accountant," Anne teased, slathering his muscled shoulders. Say what she would about golf, it had kept him trim, unlike so many men his age.

He twisted around and grabbed her hand. "Former accountant. Now I'm your full-time husband and companion in crime."

"If this is criminal activity, bring it on," Anne joked. She opened the cooler lid and got out their lunch. They sipped tea and munched on the sandwiches and chips while watching tiny waves ruffle the shore. The incessant shushing sound combined with the warm sunshine was so relaxing that Anne felt drowsy.

"Gosh, I could take a nap," she said, wrapping up the remains of her sandwich.

Davis yawned. "Me too." He took the section of blanket exposed to the sun and lay on his front, nestling into the sand to get comfortable.

Anne stayed under the umbrella, not wanting to risk a burn. Even fully under its shelter, she knew from experience that reflected light would tan her skin. She pushed the cooler aside and lay on her back, closing her eyes. A light breeze played gently over her skin and the cries of gulls accented the continuous sound of the waves.

But despite her physical comfort, sleep didn't come. Instead an urgent need to speak pressed against her breastbone, building in intensity until she could no longer bear it.

"Davis? Are you awake?"

17

Grace

Grace was in the kitchen taking an inventory of the pantry when Charlotte returned. "How'd it go?" she asked, watching as her sister unloaded two canvas bags onto the counter. Winston jumped down from his chair to investigate.

"Great." Charlotte gave a one-shouldered shrug. "I ran into Dean." She opened the refrigerator and stowed tubs of goat cheese, Winston shadowing every step. "These new cheeses will be perfect for social hour."

"Back up." Grace raised a hand. "What was that about Dean?" Charlotte's casual mention didn't fool her a bit. She snapped her fingers at Winston. "Come on, boy. Give Charlotte room to walk." He trotted reluctantly over to Grace.

Charlotte carried clear bags of produce to the sink. "I ran into him right when I got there. We had coffee then toured the market together." She sent Grace a sly grin over her shoulder. "I managed to secretly design a recipe without letting on."

"For the contest?" That was so like Charlotte, to make an uncomfortable situation into a good-humored game.

"Uh-huh." Charlotte held up a bag of chicken drumettes. "I've invented strawberry barbecue chicken." She pulled hot peppers, honey, and garlic cloves out of her bag. "With a sweet and spicy sauce. I just have to cook it up, then I'll test it on our guests this afternoon."

"That's a great plan." Grace finished the shopping list.

Charlotte nodded. She joined Grace at the counter and began

jotting down notes for her recipe. "We have wonderful guests this week, don't we? Davis and Anne seem like such a nice couple."

"They sure are." Grace hoped they were having a good day together. She went over to the coffee maker and picked up the carafe. "Coffee?"

"Sure, I'll take another cup." Charlotte tapped her pencil on the counter, thinking.

Grace slid a mug in front of Charlotte. "I'm going to stop by the chamber of commerce in a few. I'm hoping they can get the word out about the costumes. Namely, not to come here."

Charlotte laughed. "I thought I was still dreaming when I ran into that young man this morning." She told Grace about her nightmare. "He looked pretty strange flitting among the trees in the fog."

"I'll bet." Grace sipped coffee while looking over the list again. She slid it over to Charlotte. "Did I forget anything?"

Her sister studied the list and made a couple of notes, then pushed it back. "That should do it."

"Thanks. I'll go by Hanson's Farm Fresh Foods after I visit the chamber." They bought many of their bulk supplies at the locally owned grocer, who gave them a good deal. Grace located her handbag and headed for the rear door, followed by Winston. "I'll be back in a while. I'm taking Winston."

Charlotte didn't answer, and when Grace looked back she saw the chef was deep in thought. No doubt the creative wheels were turning.

Grace and Winston drove downtown to the chamber of commerce, located in a quaint and charming former train station. The town had moved the whole building next to the waterfront park, the perfect location for visitors to access information.

With some difficulty, Grace found a parking spot. Then she clipped a leash on Winston's collar and walked him over to their destination. Along the way, she noted the activity at the festival, the crowds around the booths, and the children's games going on in the park.

The chamber of commerce building looked inviting with its overflowing window boxes, bunting, and fresh coat of pale yellow and green paints. Like many train stations of the era, this one featured overhanging eaves, a wide porch, and lots of gingerbread.

Missy Perkins, the chamber director, was at the front desk talking to a family of six. Missy wore teased—and dyed—red hair in a bouffant style, bangs draped diagonally toward large green eyes adorned with false lashes.

She fluttered those lashes now as she gave directions. "Follow Lake Haven Road for three miles and the motel will be on your left. Enjoy your stay." She wiggled her fingers at the children and grinned.

They thanked her and left, jostling past Grace and Winston. Missy folded a piece of gum and popped it into her mouth. "How are you, Grace? When I went by the inn, the bunting looked perfect." Missy was always a cheerleader and encourager, something Grace appreciated.

"Glad you like it. We do too." She dug the newspaper announcement out of her bag. "Is there anything we can do about this?" She placed the paper on the blotter in front of Missy.

Missy scanned the advertisement, her fuchsia lips pursed. Her plump cheeks flamed with a color that almost matched the lipstick. "I noticed they made a mistake when the paper came out. Your inn isn't a judging station. I'm so sorry."

"Mistakes happen," Grace said. "What can we do about it? We're still getting people in costume popping in at random times. One scared Charlotte this morning, looming out of the fog."

"Oh, my. That must have been a sight." Missy laughed and shook her head. "We made the correction on social media and our website after Charlotte called. I guess it's not enough."

Grace glanced around the room, at the racks of brochures and display of local art. "How about a poster in the window with the list? And a big note that the inn is not a judging station?"

"We can do that," Missy said. "When my intern comes in this afternoon, I'll put her right on it."

"Thanks. That would be super." Grace smiled. "The festival is a marvelous success. You must be very proud."

Missy stood to walk Grace to the door. "It sure is. People are saying it's one of the best events we've done. We've got a good team, that's why."

Grace pushed the door open. "Well, keep up the good work." Missy called goodbye and she and Winston exited. "Where to now, Winston?" She'd taken care of the rooms at the inn so she could spare a little more time away before going to the grocery store. "Want to walk around and say hey to our friends?"

He panted in response, looking up at her with his big eyes.

"I'll take that as a yes." Grace strolled through the park toward the vendor booths, planning to make another circuit. She and Charlotte liked to exchange small, whimsical gifts at Christmas. Maybe she'd find something perfect, even if the holiday was seven months away.

Angel Diaz, the youngest member of The Busy Bees, was standing next to a booth filled with artwork. She waved when she spotted Grace, her long, dark hair swinging.

"How's my *chico guapo*?" Angel crooned when the duo reached the booth. She bent to give her handsome boy lots of love and Winston went nuts wagging his tail and yipping.

Grace laughed. "We were in town doing errands so I thought I'd walk around and check things out." She studied the watercolor paintings in the booth, easily identifying which were Angel's. Her work was colorful and imaginative, drawing on both her Cuban heritage and Low Country life. A small but boldly tinted painting of a rooster and sunflowers caught her eye. The jewel-like tones would look perfect in the kitchen, over the coffee nook.

"See anything you like?" Angel asked. She lowered her voice. "I'll give you the family and friends discount."

Grace continued to stare at the painting, caught by its perfection. She pointed. "I really want that."

"Good choice," Angel said. She named a price and after Grace nodded, moved to remove the painting from the exhibit. "This is the first morning I've been able to be here. My friends and I are sharing this booth and it's worked out well."

Grace looked around at the other works, mainly sculptures and woodcarving "That's a good idea, to share." Angel worked part-time at the Dragonfly Coffee Shop, which would make it hard to spend full days at the festival.

"Is Charlotte ready for the entrée contest?" Angel asked as she wrapped the painting in tissue paper. She laughed. "Everyone is trying to guess who will win, her or Dean. It will be a fight to the finish."

Grace already knew her sister was a top contender for the prize since she was a fabulous chef. And she was well aware of the rivalry Charlotte felt with Dean. But she had no idea the rest of the town saw it too.

To answer Angel, she said, "She's ready. I think she enjoys the challenge. Iron sharpening iron and all that."

Angel slid the painting into a bag with handles. "That's an appropriate analogy for chefs." Grinning, she handed the bag to Grace. "May the best cook win."

Other browsers arrived at the booth so Grace and Winston took their leave, strolling down the aisle to check out other merchandise. At one selling antique jewelry, Grace spotted Bridget O'Brien. Her guest was looking at necklaces while playing with the one she wore around her neck.

"Hi Bridget," Grace said. "Enjoying the festival?"

Bridget glanced up and for a moment, she seemed confused. "Oh, hi, Grace. I didn't recognize you for a moment."

Bridget had been lost in thought. "Not surprising," Grace said with a laugh. "I'm out of context here. Looking at jewelry?"

"Sort of." She continued to fiddle with her necklace. "I'm trying to learn more about this locket." She held it out so Grace could see. "It was, uh, passed down to me and I was hoping to learn more about its possible origins."

Bridget was from Boston, Grace knew. "You think it came from the South?"

The other woman cocked her head, giving Grace a wry smile. "I think *I* did."

A few minutes later they were seated at a picnic table under a tree, drinking tall iced teas. A folk duo on the bandstand was performing "Puff the Magic Dragon" to the delight of a group of dancing toddlers.

Bridget sipped on her straw. "I'm starting to really like sweet tea."

"It's the nectar of the gods," Grace said. "We drink gallons of it." After Bridget's revelation a few minutes ago, Grace was letting her drive the conversation.

"You're probably wondering what I was talking about," Bridget said as the singers gave yet another rendition of the chorus. "I was adopted. And from what my adoptive mother told me, I believe my birth parents came from Magnolia Harbor."

Grace's curiosity was sparked by this surprising statement. Although Bridget was almost a decade younger, Grace might well know her parents, if they still lived in town. "What did she say exactly?"

Bridget's eyes grew thoughtful. "It was near the end of her life, when she was really ill." She blinked back tears. "Mom was a wonderful woman. I still miss her." After swallowing, she continued, "Anyway, one day she said, 'You've been the light of our lives, Bree.' She always called me Bree. 'Adopting you was the best thing we ever did. What a brave choice your birth mother made.' I'd never pressed too hard on the subject of my birth parents since I sensed it upset them. But since she brought her up, I asked if she knew anything about her. Mom shook her head. 'The adoption was closed, and back then they didn't tell you anything. All I know is, she came from a little town in South Carolina called Magnolia Harbor. The person we were dealing with shouldn't have even said that. It was a slip of the tongue, because Dick was talking about his connections to the area. That's how we found the agency.'"

Grace focused on her tea, giving Bridget a minute to compose herself. She noticed that the faint air of stress her guest carried seemed to have dissolved. Maybe talking about her situation was making her feel better, less burdened.

Bridget's hand went to her necklace. "Besides what Mom said, I have only this locket." She held it out so Grace could read the engraving. "See? It says *Lula*."

"It belonged to your birth mother?" Grace admired the finely wrought silver. She could tell at a glance it was of good quality.

"I think so." Bridget smoothed the necklace back into place with a pat. "Or my father." She paused. "The odd thing is, I saw this exact same locket at the Jackson House Museum. Olympia Jackson was wearing it in a portrait."

"Did Olympia have children?" Grace asked. Although she'd grown up here, she didn't recall any. She hadn't even been acquainted with Olympia, who, if she recalled, had been reclusive. She must have died before Grace returned to Magnolia Harbor and bought the inn.

"I don't know. If my mom is alive, I figure she's in her very late fifties to early sixties. I'll be forty-two this year."

Bridget's mother was more than a decade older than Grace, then. Grace would have been about five when Bridget was born, too young to know many kids beyond her kindergarten or first-grade class.

"I'm hoping Julep can help me," Bridget said. "I met her at the library and she invited me to tea tomorrow."

"Julep Buckley? She used to run the historical society, so if anyone knows anything, it's Julep." Grace had benefited from the historian's formidable knowledge when filling gaps in the inn's history.

"That's what Phyllis said." Bridget took the last sip of her tea. "I guess I'm ready to head back to the inn. I'm going to try to do some writing this afternoon."

"Did you come down on the shuttle?" Grace remembered seeing Bridget's rental car still parked at the inn. "I can give you a ride." Then she remembered. "Or maybe not. I have to stop by the market and pick up some groceries."

Bridget placed her hands on the picnic table and stood. "I don't mind. I like browsing in grocery stores when I travel." Grace must have revealed her surprise because Bridget added, "I enjoy learning about regional differences in brands and food choices. It makes me a better writer."

Grace thought about some of the food that might fall into the category of different for a Boston girl and smiled. Pimiento cheese. Fried okra. Sorghum syrup. "Let's go."

An hour later, they pulled into the inn drive. "I need to go around back," Grace said, "so I can unload. Want me to let you out in front?"

Bridget shook her head. "Let me help you. It's the least I can do after that field trip." Her guest had a bag of packaged Southern snacks she was going to sample. And if she liked them, she planned to take some home for her daughter and husband.

When they walked, laden with bags, into the kitchen, Charlotte looked up from washing vegetables in the sink. "We have a new guest," she said, breaking into a big smile.

Grace set her bags down. "But we're full. Did someone check out?"

Charlotte shook her head. "Bridget, you might want to go say hello. Our new guest is on the back veranda."

Bridget put a hand to her chest. "Me?" She glanced back and forth between the sisters. "I don't understand what's going on, but okay." She hurried out of the kitchen, followed by Grace a few steps behind.

When Grace reached the porch, she saw Bridget embracing a tall, burly man with thinning curly red hair and twinkling blue eyes. She let go of the man and beamed at her hostess. "Grace, I'd like you to meet my husband, Sean."

18

Bridget

Bridget's heart soared with joy. She hadn't realized exactly how much she'd missed her husband until she saw him seated on the inn's veranda, leafing through a magazine. Slipping her arm through his, she asked, "I can't get over how you surprised me this way. I had no idea."

Smiling down at her, Sean patted her hand. "Molly gave me a push to do it. I have a lot of earned time off so it wasn't a problem to duck out for few days."

Molly. Longing for her daughter pierced Bridget. "Who's taking care of Molly?" She might not need a babysitter but she couldn't stay alone at night. Not for another few years.

"I got my mom to come over." He patted her hand again. "I left them baking brownies and gearing up for an epic game of rummy."

After excusing herself, Grace had slipped back inside. Bridget hoped the innkeeper wouldn't mind that Bridget wasn't helping with the rest of the groceries, although she had a feeling Grace understood.

"Want to see my—I mean, our room?" Bridget asked. "It's really nice."

"Sure. I left my bag in the front hall." Sean stood back to let her enter the house first and followed her down the hallway to the foyer. "This place is magnificent."

"Isn't it? I feel so comfortable here," Bridget said. She saw Sean's leather satchel sitting by the stairs. "I'm on the third floor." He picked up the bag and together they went up to the Wisteria Loft Suite.

"Ta-da," Bridget said, throwing the door open wide. While Sean lugged his bag inside and found a luggage rack to set it on, she buzzed around, displaying all the suite's features.

"Not too shabby," Sean said, joining her on the veranda. "Look at that lake." He lifted his face to the warm breeze. "Man, it's at least twenty degrees colder at home right now."

"I'll bet." Right now Boston felt very, very far away to Bridget. She could barely imagine its gray grit, the noise of traffic, the grind of constant, joyless movement.

"Want a sweet tea?" she asked, darting back into the room. "They've become my addiction." She retrieved two bottles from the small room refrigerator.

By the time she returned to the veranda, Sean was planted in one of the wide, comfortable chairs. He accepted the bottle, twisted off the cap and drank.

Bridget laughed at his wide eyes. "I know. All that sugar takes getting used to."

"You're my sugar," Sean said in a credible imitation of a Southern accent. "I'm dying to know, how's the book going?"

She put up a hand with a laugh. "First, tell me how things are at home. How did Molly do on that science test?"

Sean's grin was smug. "Aced it." He patted his chest with one broad hand. "After her old man tutored her. It's like she convinces herself she can't do it."

Bridget thought about her own school days. "That sounds familiar. I had a phobia about certain subjects so I psyched myself out." She still shivered when someone said the word geometry.

"Kids do that with English," Sean said. "They freak out about making it perfect. That's why I try to get them to loosen up with free writing. Then we worry about punctuation, spelling, and so forth."

"You're a great teacher." Admiration for her husband warmed

Bridget. Although he didn't teach for the kudos, he'd won his fair share of awards and recognition. But what meant the most to Sean were thank-you notes from graduates. Even in an era of spell-check and other tools, being able to write well was critical for college success. Some expressed fervent gratitude when they later realized how well Mr. O'Brien had prepared them.

He brushed off the compliment, as typical, his blue eyes studying her with warm affection. "We have a good life, Bree, you know that? But once in a while it needs to be about us. Spend some quality time together, as they say."

His statement so closely paralleled Bridget's recent thoughts about priorities that she gasped. "I was thinking that last night. You must have read my mind." They were always in tune, had been since the beginning.

Another thought struck. More of a stab to the heart, really. Why had she kept the search for her birth parents from Sean? *What was she thinking?* He was her partner, her mate, her best friend.

Repentant tears burned her eyes. "Oh, Sean." Her voice got that choked, high-pitched quality it always did when she was going to cry.

Alarm flashed over his features, wiping away his tender smile. "What is it, Bree? You're not sick, are you?" His brow knotted in concern.

"No, I'm not sick." Bridget paused to search around for a tissue, since her nose was running. Another lovely side effect of crying.

"Then what is it?" Sean fished in his pocket and pulled out clean, folded tissues. He always carried them. Handing them over, he said, "Put me out of my misery, will you?"

Bridget wiped her eyes and nose. "I didn't come to Magnolia Harbor just to work on the book. Though it's been excellent for that." She paused to inhale. With every word, the selfish absurdity of keeping her secret became clearer. "Something Mom said before she passed made me think my birth mother grew up here. Or was living here when she had me."

Sean seemed to absorb this, then nodded. "So you thought you'd kill two birds with one stone. I get it." His brow knotted again. "But you could have told me." He made a disbelieving grunt. "You know I'd never stand in the way of you learning about your family."

"I do know that." Bridget ran a hand through her hair, pushing it off her forehead. "I—I guess I didn't want to disappoint you—and Molly—if it was a dead end."

His eyes grew soft. "Disappoint us? I don't think that's it."

The truth of his gentle words hit home. Bridget had been trying to protect *herself*. As long as her loved ones didn't know about her quest, she could almost pretend it didn't really matter.

But it did. Oh, how it mattered. Bridget's heart twisted in agony, and for the first time she allowed herself to truly feel the loss, pain, and rejection she carried. A kernel of hurt had formed the day she learned she was adopted. From then on, no matter how often she reassured herself that Mom and Dad loved her, she knew the truth. *Her real mother hadn't wanted her.*

"Oh, Sean." This time the tears were fast and furious. Her husband gathered her to his chest, held her tenderly in his arms, soothing and murmuring, stroking her hair.

"We'll find her, Bree," he whispered. "I promise."

Bridget felt for the locket and held it loosely in her hand. "But I might be at a dead end." She thought of Julep. Would she have answers for her?

He kissed her hair. "That was before I got here."

She knew his statement was joking bravado, meant to make her laugh. So she did. Then she said, "I hope you're right. We can do anything together, can't we, Sean?"

19

Anne

"I'm here, honey," Davis said, his voice soft and eager. Then his phone rang.

A snort of hysterical laughter burst out of Anne. *Three guesses.* Here she'd finally been ready to talk, worked herself up to it, and Cora somehow picked this moment to call.

The phone continued to ring. Davis rolled onto his side and glanced over at her. "Is it . . . do you mind if I take this? Mother was supposed to have some kind of test."

Resentment knotted Anne's chest but she shook her head. How could she say no? Although why his mother scheduled a medical test this week, she had no idea. There had been no mention of it before they left, and she certainly wasn't having a medical emergency. If she was, Cora would probably have the news broadcast on the highway signs along their route. *Turn back, Davis, your mother needs you.*

Still talking, Davis levered himself to his feet and began trudging through the sand. Hot irritation burned. Why did he always talk to Cora in private, as though he needed to hide their conversation? It had always been that way, the proverbial fly in the ointment of their marriage.

A situation she'd used to justify keeping secrets, she realized uncomfortably.

Then annoyance rose afresh at seeing her husband stop walking with his back to her. Davis and Cora. Mother and son, cozy in a private club that excluded Anne. Always had. From the day she'd met the woman who would become her mother-in-law.

After dating several months, Davis had invited her to the Montgomery home, pretentiously named Montgomery Manor. Oh, it was large enough, a six-bedroom mansion in a nice housing development, but still. *Who names their house?* Anne remembered wondering.

Leroy Montgomery was still alive then, and he was courtly and charming, a real Southern gentleman. He'd welcomed her with open arms. As for Cora, well, it was very apparent that she wasn't pleased with Davis's choice.

Especially when he revealed that they were already thinking about marriage. After that, the claws went in a bit but Cora made it a point to grill Anne about her family. Discreetly, of course. Anne was at a real disadvantage since she had created a new, false identity. An orphan with no connections.

She still remembered that first dinner, which she endured with clammy hands and a pounding heart, so afraid she'd say the wrong thing. She hadn't been able to swallow a bite of the meal prepared by Cora's cook. Even now, forty years later, the sight of chicken cordon bleu made her feel ill. Those rolls of pale meat wrapped around ham and cheese, topped with an oily sauce—ugh.

What was immediately apparent was that Anne could do no right in Cora's eyes. And later on, when Anne was introduced into their social circle, she figured out why.

Cora had earmarked her best friend's daughter, gorgeous, gracious Belinda Bell, for Davis. Belinda never put a foot wrong, Anne had thought. When the two of them became friends, bonding over their sons and the frustrations and joys of young married life, she learned differently. Belinda was human, after all. Belinda didn't care for her mother-in-law either, who was equally critical of her son's bride. They had fun trading stories and both felt supported as a result.

Walking bowlegged like a sailor in the soft sand, Davis returned to the blanket, the phone resting in his hand. Mercifully the call had ended fairly quickly. They'd been known to go on for over an hour.

Anne had planned to ask Davis how his mother was, since she always swallowed her exasperation and tried to be supportive. Maybe Cora really was sick this time, although every other ailment had turned out to be imaginary, rather than an actual condition.

But from a faraway little corner of her mind, she saw herself leap up. Watched as she clenched her fists and gritted her teeth. Felt a lightning bolt of anger galvanize her core.

"Anne. What's wrong?" Her husband looked almost comically alarmed.

Her response was a growl. She took a step forward and felt her bare foot hit something sharp, but kept going. "Davis," she ground out. "How much longer is your mother going to run our lives? Interrupt our time together?"

He took a step backward, confusion shadowing his eyes. "What do you mean? She doesn't—she's old, she needs—"

Anne took another step, dimly aware that her right foot was bleeding. "She's been that way since she was forty-two, when I met her. You're still her *little boy*, aren't you?" She heard the jeering note in her voice and winced. There was no need to be cruel and nasty. Part of her knew it wasn't all about her husband and his mother. They were only the scapegoats for her confused, painful feelings about her own parent.

For a fleeting second, she could see herself from his point of view, a scowling harpy on a rampage. But then anger, frustration, and pain swallowed her like a huge wave. She swayed on her feet, buffeted by emotion, a current of relief running under it all. She had kept the resentment in for so long, it felt remarkably good to release it.

His face resembled stone, jaw set, brow rigid. "Is that how you really feel, Anne?"

Yes. No. She rested her hands on her hips. "Yep. Davis and Cora, party of two."

Davis sagged, his shoulders slumping. "Why are you doing this, Anne?" he said. "Why now? We were having a good time, despite . . . despite everything."

Because my mother didn't love me. And I'm jealous.

Anne gasped, this new awareness slapping her like cold water. Yes, Cora was a pain, self-centered and critical. But she loved her son, no one could deny that. And her grandson too, Anne's son.

Anne crumpled to the sand and put her hands over her face. She *had* ruined everything. Davis would hate her now, want a divorce—

A warm hand rested on her arm. "Annie? Darling? You're killing me here." His voice was pleading, revealing a vulnerability she rarely glimpsed.

He isn't angry, he's hurt. This realization flooded her with remorse. She gazed up at her husband's face, her vision blurred with tears. "My . . . my mother was nothing like yours." Her voice shook but she swallowed hard and continued. "I've always felt left out, alone, unwanted. But to be fair, it started in my own home, not ours."

He lowered himself to the ground beside her. "Talk to me, Annie." He kissed the side of her head. "Tell your Davis all about it."

Where to start? Why not at the beginning? "You know that picture of your mother hugging you when you were a baby?" Her voice cracked. "You can just see the love all over her, she was so proud." She swallowed. "Mama never hugged me. Or kissed me. Or said she loved me." She gulped in air, feeling as if she were about to jump off a high dive and might hit the rocks below. "She wasn't married when she had me. I ruined her life. And she never forgave me for it."

20

Charlotte

Visions were dancing through Charlotte's head as she dreamily hulled quarts of strawberries at the sink. Ever since the concept for her new cookbook, *Comfort and Cheer at the Magnolia Harbor Inn,* had floated into her mind, she'd been flooded with inspiration. She could see the finished book, the glossy pages filled with lovely photographs of the inn, tables laden with delicious, mouth-watering dishes . . .

"How's it going?" Grace's voice broke into her daydream. Winston at her heels, she carried a basket of creamy white roses and lilies to the table.

Charlotte pointed her knife at the flowers. "Are any red roses in bloom?"

Grace opened a cabinet and pulled out a vase, while Winston jumped onto a nearby chair and curled up, watching her every movement. "That's a strange response, but yes, there are a few."

"Sorry." Charlotte laughed. "I've been planning my new cookbook." *Instead of finalizing the contest entry recipe.* She held up a strawberry. "I thought we could stage a shortcake picture today. A few vases of red and white flowers would look awesome on the table, like we did for the social." Her publisher would send another photographer later, once the cookbook was written, but she liked to put her own spin on the visuals. They could use Grace's shots on social media to promote the inn and build buzz for the book.

"How about setting up on the veranda?" Grace asked. "We could position the table so the magnolia trees are in the background." She put the vase back and chose another. "I'll do arrangements of different heights."

"Perfect." Her sister often had an uncanny ability to bring Charlotte's visions to life. "That's what I was imagining."

The timer buzzed so Charlotte set down the knife and hurried toward the oven. She slipped on mitts and pulled out a tray of tall, delicately browned biscuits. At Winston's raised nose and sniff, Charlotte wagged a scolding finger. "These aren't for you, Winston. Although if you're lucky, there might be a dropped crumb or two later."

Grace rummaged around in the cupboard, glass clinking. "I thought you were working on your barbecue chicken recipe for the contest."

"I am." With a spatula, Charlotte deftly removed the shortcakes from the pan and placed them on a cooling rack. "But as I was preparing strawberries for the sauce, I realized we should do the shortcake photo shoot now. Why waste these great berries?"

"Good point. We can also mention they were locally grown and give Roy Bevins a plug." Grace held up a cut-glass dessert bowl with scalloped edges. "How about using these?" The bowl was an antique, one of four their mother had passed down.

"Sure. We can put whole strawberries in the matching serving bowl." Cut glass dishes, real, heavy silver, and a white linen cloth would all look beautiful and elegant together. Another idea sparked. "Let's do a section in the book called 'Summer Supper.'"

"I like it," Grace declared. "What other dishes will you include?"

"I hadn't gotten that far." Charlotte tapped a foot, thinking. "Something grilled of course, cold salads, maybe." Images swirled in her mind, followed by sensations of taste and aroma. She'd learned that a successful cookbook appealed to all the senses. Not literally, but through the power of memory and the imagination. "I know. We'll do a home salad bar."

"That will showcase the individual ingredients," Grace said. "All local as well, right?"

"Of course. Lettuce, beets, peas, cucumber, tomatoes . . . all in contrasting pottery bowls." Charlotte whirled back to the sink. She picked the plumpest, reddest strawberries out of the batch and set them in a colander. These would remain whole for the photo, both in the cut-glass bowl and spilling out artistically on the tablecloth.

Winnie entered the kitchen, her gaze falling on the vases and basket of flowers. "Need a hand?"

Charlotte pivoted to smile at her aunt. "Sure do. Want to help Grace set a table on the veranda? We're staging a shot for my new cookbook."

"New cookbook?" Winnie clasped her hands together, her eyes lighting up with interest. "Tell me more."

Charlotte gave her a brief description while slicing strawberries, tossing less-than-perfect ones into a pot for the barbecue sauce.

Winnie made suitably impressed noises. "I love the concept," she declared. "It will really promote the inn too. Everyone will want to stay here."

"That's what I thought," Charlotte said, gratified. A pulse of excitement beat in her veins. This was so much better than working as a chef in a restaurant owned by someone else. There she served only at management's whim, no matter how talented she was or how hard she worked. At Magnolia Harbor Inn, all her efforts helped build the business, and she, Grace and Winnie benefited.

Grace and Winnie bustled out to the veranda with the flowers and vases while Charlotte whipped fresh cream. Once the table was ready, she'd put together the shortcakes. Until then, it was time to stop stalling and make the barbecue sauce. One of her problems had been settling on the final recipe. But she had a built-in group of testers. Why not try several variations on the main theme and then let the guests weigh in?

Relieved by that decision, another idea trickled into her mind. Speaking of building buzz, why not do that for her Strawberry Fest contest entry? She took out her phone and snapped a deliberately out-of-focus picture of ingredients on the counter with the gas range in the background.

She couldn't suppress a giggle as she uploaded the post. Hopefully people would be curious and come out in droves to try—and vote for—her recipe.

"What are you laughing about?" Grace asked as she walked into the kitchen, a smile spreading across her face.

"Oh, nothing," Charlotte answered, still gazing at her phone. People were already reading her post, marking it with hearts and thumbs-up icons. "I'm promoting the contest, that's all."

Grace's gaze flicked toward the array of ingredients on the counter. "Did you figure out your sauce?"

Charlotte tucked the phone away. "Almost. I'm still developing it." She pursed her lips and moved a bottle of balsamic vinegar over an inch. Salty, sweet, and tangy, the trio of flavor notes that made a great barbecue sauce. A little cayenne or jalapeno to give an extra kick.

"If you're at a good point to stop, want to come see what we did?" Grace stepped backward, gesturing toward the veranda.

"Sure. I'd love to." Charlotte smoothed her apron and hurried after her sister, pushing aside the vague, unsettled feeling she always got while creating new dishes. It would all come together eventually. She just needed to have faith.

On the veranda, a table had been moved to the exact corner Grace mentioned. In the foreground, three vases held lush, casual arrangements. A blooming magnolia tree provided a beautiful backdrop in the distance.

"I'm thinking we can set the dishes of shortcake here," Grace said, tapping an empty space on the table. They'd already laid out silver spoons and cloth napkins on the thick, snowy cloth.

"And how about putting a pitcher of iced tea over here?" Winnie asked. "With four of those tall, etched glasses?" She was referring to a set of antiques housed in a dining room cabinet.

"I love it," Charlotte said. She squinted, evaluating the afternoon sunlight and shadows. The indirect light was perfect right now. "While you get your camera set up, Grace, I'll put together the shortcakes." Grace used a tripod for staged pictures to ensure the shots were sharp.

"And I'll get the iced tea ready," Winnie said. "You have some in the fridge, I noticed, so I just need to fill a pitcher and add ice."

Footsteps sounded on the veranda boards and a moment later, Curt came around the corner. His steps stuttered. "Oh, I'm sorry. I didn't know you were busy out here."

"You're okay," Grace said. "We're getting ready to shoot photographs for Charlotte's new cookbook."

Winnie patted his forearm. "Why don't you have a seat and I'll bring you some tea?"

Curt sat in a rocker, then shifted and pulled something out of his pocket. He set a small, black velvet box on the table beside him.

"What's that you've got there, Curt?" Grace's smile was teasing.

He picked the box up and fiddled with it, red flushing his cheeks. "Oh, a little something I bought for Presley." His face flamed even brighter. "Is it okay if she comes to the social hour tonight?"

Charlotte knew she should go back inside and prepare those shortcakes, but she was too curious to leave. That box was about the right size for a ring. *An engagement ring?* Not that Charlotte was any kind of expert, but she sensed a discussion of marriage was too much, too soon for the pair.

Winnie took a step forward, then halted. The line between her aunt's brows told Charlotte that she shared her concern. But she merely pressed her lips together, her eyes troubled.

"Of course Presley is welcome," Grace said, breaking the silence. "She can help test Charlotte's contest entry." Grace sent Charlotte a glance. "She's been working on a new recipe all day."

Sort of. "That's right," Charlotte said. "I'd love to have Presley's opinion. I'm going to test three barbecue sauces tonight. Y'all get to vote for your favorite."

Fifteen minutes before serving time, the chicken sizzling on the stovetop grill was ready. Using tongs, Charlotte moved the perfectly glazed drumettes to three serving platters. She'd created sweet, spicy, and spicy-sweet sauces, all with the same basic ingredients but different intensities.

She was fortunate to have guinea pigs—er, guests, to test recipes on. Usually it was Grace and Winnie on whom she experimented, along with Winnie's husband, Gus. The man always enjoyed a good meal and knew how to give helpful criticism.

As if conjured by her thoughts, she heard whistling drifting from the dining room and a moment later, Gus appeared in the kitchen doorway. "Heard you needed my expert opinion tonight," he said, his eyes twinkling behind glasses. He patted his belly in anticipation.

"Uncle Gus." Charlotte flew across the kitchen, still holding the tongs, and gave him a big hug. "I haven't seen you in ages, seems like."

"You've been busy, I hear," he said. "Full house." He pushed his glasses into place with a thumb. "I've been kind of busy myself." An air of expectation lit his face as he waited for her reaction.

"Doing what, Uncle Gus?" Charlotte returned to the chicken, removing the last few pieces from the heat. They smelled and looked good, at least, browned but still juicy.

Gus perched on a stool. "I'm building a model railroad, a reproduction of one of the defunct local lines." Gus was a retired train conductor. "I'm creating little vignettes too. Bridges, ocean, little towns."

Charlotte rescued a runaway drumette with the tongs. "It sounds wonderful. I'll have to come over and see it."

Grace bustled into the kitchen, glancing at the clock. "Anne and Davis aren't going to make it. They just got on the island ferry." She noticed Gus and detoured toward him for a hug. "Good to see you, Gus. Keeping busy?"

"Oh, I sure am." He launched into a description of his model railroad while the sisters and Winnie put together serving dishes for the social. Besides the tiny pieces of chicken, they were offering assorted crudités with ranch dip, potato puffs, and a selection of cheese and crackers.

"Yum," Gus said, grabbing a puff as Winnie carried them by. "You ladies sure know how to cook."

"That's the idea, Uncle Gus," Charlotte said. Now that the moment was upon her, she realized she was a little nervous. She thought the sauces tasted good and hopefully her testers would agree. But most important of all, was her new recipe good enough to best the other entries—namely Dean Bradley's?

Bridget and her husband Sean were first of the guests to appear, holding hands like a couple newly in love. Charlotte smiled. The Magnolia Harbor Inn was a special place, that was for sure.

"What do we have here?" Bridget asked, peering at the food while Sean watched fondly. "It all looks so good." She placed a potato puff on a plate.

"There are a few choices, but I'd especially love for you to sample each of these sauces and tell me which one you prefer." Charlotte pointed to A, B, and C cards behind the dishes.

"Test taste?" Sean guessed, picking up a plate. He rubbed his midriff. "I'm in."

Bridget rolled her eyes with a smile. "As long as it's edible, Sean's your man."

"I can recommend all three," Gus called, halfway through a piece of chicken. He and Winnie were seated on chairs to one side, a high-piled plate placed on an occasional table between them.

"Try to narrow it down, Uncle," Charlotte said. "I can only enter one recipe."

Gus chuckled and picked up another piece of chicken. "Tough job but someone's got to do it. Who would have thought strawberry barbecue sauce would be so good?"

"It's addicting," Winnie said.

"Are you entering the strawberry entrée contest later this week?" Bridget asked. "I remember hearing about that." She chose one piece of each flavor, as requested.

"She sure is," Grace said from behind the wine station. "Charlotte hopes to win."

"I bet that would be good for the inn," Sean said. He moved along behind Bridget, filling his plate.

"It sure would," Charlotte said with a grin. "Plus it'll be fun." *Fun to see Dean's face when he loses.* Maybe she'd arrange a bet with him. Loser gets to take the winner out for dinner at the place of his or her choice.

After accepting glasses of white wine from Grace, the couple from Boston sat down near Gus and Winnie. The foursome was soon chatting away, the talk punctuated by bellows of laughter from the men. "C wins," Sean called at one point. "Sweet *and* spicy, right?" He winked and gave Charlotte a thumbs-up. "It rocks." The others murmured in agreement.

"Thanks, everyone." Charlotte put a finger to her lips. "Remember, it's a secret. I don't want anyone else to scoop me." They all agreed to keep Charlotte's secret.

Grace sidled over to Charlotte. "I wonder if anyone else is coming down."

Charlotte rearranged the chicken pieces on the plates. "I hope so. We made tons." It sounded like C had won but she would love a few more votes before the final decision.

"Here come Curt and Presley." Grace elbowed Charlotte. The pair was wandering arm in arm through the gardens, headed toward the rose garden.

Charlotte didn't blame them. With more bushes coming into bloom each day, there wasn't a more romantic spot on the property.

Presley bent to smell a pink rose, then turned to Curt with a laugh. They were too far away to hear the words, but whatever she said made Curt laugh in response.

To Charlotte's amazement, Curt dropped to one knee right there in the grass, ring box in hand. His upturned face was earnest and handsome, a lock of hair falling across his brow.

It was a picture perfect proposal, except for one flaw—the reaction of the prospective bride. Oh, she put both hands to her face in surprise, as might be expected, but instead of smiling and saying yes, she barked something at her suitor and stormed off.

21

Anne

The evening sun lay low over the water, tinting it orange and gold. Below the deck where Anne and Davis stood, a creamy wake marked the ferry's passage.

Anne leaned against the metal railing, feeling battered and bruised, every muscle in her body aching. That was more to do with going through the emotional wringer, she knew, rather than the day's activities. As for her state of mind, she was numb, drained, depleted. Each revelation as they'd sunned on the beach, eaten lunch, and toured the island had released a bit of the burden, like taking down a wall brick by brick.

Davis was the first person she'd ever spoken to about her past, she realized. An only child, she had no siblings. And one of Mama's rules was that dirty laundry was never aired outside the home. For that matter, it was barely acknowledged inside. So that eliminated school chums and adult acquaintances as possible confidants.

Besides, what would she tell them? That she was Mama's secret shame, something she paid the price for every day she drew breath? The fact she'd told Davis and he still loved and accepted her felt like a miracle, the one she'd prayed for.

So far so good. There was more to tell, much more, but she'd taken a huge step today.

"So your dad was never in the picture?" Davis asked. "That's shameful on his part." Davis had been blessed with a wonderful father, and he was one in turn. Cora might rule the roost, but Leroy Montgomery was the stalwart foundation supporting the family—quiet, usually in the background, but always there.

Anne examined her husband's face. He'd been stalwart himself today, unflinching as she described each ugly episode of her life.

"I've never met him. For a long time, Mama said she was divorced and had taken back her name. But I figured it out." Anne recalled the hours she'd spent in the dusty attic searching through trunks and musty cardboard boxes.

Her mother's indifference had resulted in Anne seeking information about her father. In the back of her mind, she'd had a fantasy that he would come and take her away to live with him. Maybe he didn't know how Mama was. Maybe Mama had refused to let him see his daughter. She pictured a handsome, laughing man with hair and eyes like hers.

Her palms grew clammy as she remembered that particular day, the day her dreams dissolved like spun sugar in the rain. She'd been digging through a box filled with letters, postcards, and other household papers. Near the bottom, in an unmarked envelope, was a birth certificate.

She'd been born in Raleigh, she realized. Where her mother attended college. And in the space for her father's name was the cold indictment: "Unknown."

Chill seeped into her core even now as she told Davis about finding the certificate, her words stumbling as she forced them out. She couldn't meet his eyes. Imagine if Cora found out? The fact that Anne was illegitimate would only justify her distaste for her son's choice. That generation was so intolerant of "mistakes." It was so different now, thankfully.

"Oh, Anne." Davis slung his arm around her shoulders and pulled her close. "That's horrible. Why didn't she put his name down?"

Anne tried to laugh. The view of the bay was blurry through her tears. "I don't know. I'm sure she knew who he was. But she probably didn't want him to have any claim on me. That's what I'm guessing." And what a loss it had been, to not have her father in her life. She'd been bitterly envious whenever she'd seen little girls with doting dads.

Davis pulled her even closer, put both arms around her. She leaned her head on his strong shoulder. "I think we've talked about this enough for one day. I can tell it's taking a toll on you."

His thoughtfulness made the tears come faster. She kissed his warm neck. "Oh, Davis. I love you. Thank you for understanding." Sniffing, she wiped her eyes with her jacket sleeve.

"Of course," he murmured. "I had no idea you were carrying all this. I'm so sorry."

Anne nestled against his shoulder. "When I left home, I wanted a clean start. I wanted to be loved and accepted for who I was, out from under my mother's shadow."

When she glanced up at his profile, she saw he looked pensive. "I've made a few mistakes, Anne, especially regarding my mother." He chuckled. "She is quite overbearing sometimes, I admit, kind of like a human bulldozer."

Anne laughed. That was a very good description of Cora, not that her mother-in-law would appreciate it. The ferry was slowing now as it approached the mainland. The aroma of grilling meat drifted over the water from restaurants near the docks.

She was suddenly starving. "You know what I have a craving for? Soft-shell crabs." The delectable morsels, one of her favorite treats, happened to be in season.

"Then let's go get us some." Davis grinned.

After a fantastic dinner on the docks, Anne and Davis drove back to Magnolia Harbor. For the first time, the little town felt like home again. Anne enjoyed checking out the festival as the car crawled along

Lake Haven Road, Davis extra cautious due to all the pedestrians crossing. The rides were lit up, bright against an indigo sky, and music drifted from the bandstand.

"It's a hopping little place," Davis said. "Want to stop for an ice cream?" The soft serve booth had a line three deep.

Anne squeezed his hand, which she'd been holding ever since they got off the highway. She was still full from dinner. "Not right now. Rain check?" Sharing her family history had done the opposite of what she'd long feared. Instead of driving them apart, she felt closer to Davis than she had in years.

Of course that might change, once he knew the *whole* story. A jolt of fear hit her belly and she let go of his hand. With an effort, she tried to shove down the familiar sensation of guilt and heartache.

He sensed the change in her mood. "It's been a long day, Annie. We'll talk some more tomorrow, or whenever you're ready."

She leaned over and kissed his cheek. "You're the best husband in the whole world."

Davis chuckled. "I try."

They turned into the inn driveway, and at the sight of cheerful lights beckoning ahead, Anne relaxed, releasing her burdens. There was nothing quite like the sunbaked, bone-deep exhaustion of a day at the shore. Her hair and skin were stiff with salt, and when she licked her lips, she could taste it. A hot shower was definitely on the agenda.

Grace strolled out into the lobby as they entered. "Good evening. How was your day?"

"It was wonderful," Anne said. "Daufuskie Island is a must-see." That was certainly true.

"Isn't it?" Grace continued to the front door, which she locked. "Would you like to join us out back for hot cocoa? We're also toasting marshmallows. Both are homemade."

Anne glanced at Davis, who said, "It's up to you, darling. I wouldn't mind a bedtime snack."

She discovered she wouldn't either—apparently Grace's offerings were more tempting than ice cream at the festival. "All right, let's do it." To Grace she said, "We'll drop off our things upstairs and be right down."

Up in their room, Anne washed her face and brushed her hair and teeth, which made her feel a little less disheveled. *Showering could wait half an hour,* she thought. Davis cleaned up too and then they headed into the backyard.

Along with Grace and Charlotte, Curt and Bridget were standing near the brick fire pit. Another man stood beside Bridget. "Hi guys," Bridget said as they joined the others. "Have you met my husband?"

"I don't think I've had the pleasure," Davis said, extending a hand. He introduced Anne and himself, while Sean did the same.

Sean seemed nice, a good partner for Bridget. She could tell by their body language that the couple was close. Attuned to each other somehow.

Were she and Davis like that? Hopefully. Davis nudged her elbow and handed her a stick with two marshmallows already loaded, which made her laugh. There was proof for you.

Anne held the stick over the coals, laughing when one marshmallow caught fire. She quickly pulled it out and blew on the flames. She pulled the gooey mess off the stick and ate it in one bite, black bits and all.

"I like them burned," Sean said. "To a crisp." He held up his stick in demonstration.

Bridget rotated her stick exactly ninety degrees. "Not me. I toast them to perfection." She kissed her fingers like a chef. After another half minute, she rotated it again.

Curt was the only person not joining the general chitchat. He stood watching the fire, now and then nudging the coals with a poker as the self-appointed keeper of the pit. Anne found herself studying the young man, sensing the gloom that lay over him like a cloak. He was in town to see a former girlfriend, she remembered hearing. Had she rejected him, perhaps?

Bridget and Sean soon excused themselves, along with Charlotte, who mentioned the unearthly hour she rose to make breakfast. The remaining foursome refilled mugs with the creamiest, richest hot chocolate Anne had ever tasted, then sat in lounge chairs on the lawn to watch the stars come out.

Anne was seated beside Curt, who sipped from his mug in silence. If he was upset, and it sure seemed that way to her, why was he still lingering? She thought of her son's behavior and knew the answer. He wanted to talk but didn't know how to broach the topic.

"How are you, Curt?" she asked. A short distance away, Grace and Davis were talking about the route they'd taken around the island. It sounded like Davis was giving her a blow-by-blow itinerary.

"I've been better," Curt said, his tone ironic. He gave a bitter laugh. "Ask Grace. She saw the whole thing." Grace glanced over but turned her attention back to Davis.

Anne waited, not wanting to probe, a technique that worked with Austin more times than not. She was soon rewarded by a snort.

Curt slumped forward, resting his elbows on his knees. "I kind of jumped the gun with Presley. I asked her to marry me—again—and she told me off."

Oh my. Anne winced. Her heart went out to the young man. What a painful reaction to what should have been a happy event. "Any idea why?" Davis came over to sit beside Anne and she threw him a quick smile.

"Maybe." Curt pushed the toe of his loafer into the soft grass. "From what she said, she felt like I was being too domineering. Trying to go too fast." He groaned and scrubbed his hands over his face. "It wouldn't be the first time."

Anne had no comment regarding Curt's supposed personality flaws. But she did send up a silent wish for the couple and searched for the right words to say. After a moment, she said, "Curt, it's apparent you love Presley. Tell her that, and apologize for jumping the gun. Tell her that if she'll give you another chance, you'll let her set the pace. But don't push for an answer. Give her time to think about it, if she needs it."

Curt still didn't meet her eyes. But he said, "Good advice. Since I'm only in town for a few days, I've felt pressure to make things happen." His laugh was tinged with bitter humor. "I guess I thought I'd come back and she'd fall at my feet in gratitude. Maybe her calling me arrogant isn't so far off the mark after all." He turned to Davis. "Tell me, what's the secret of a long and happy marriage?"

His question jolted Anne and she held her breath, waiting to hear her husband's answer. Davis reached for her hand. "I don't have all the answers, son," Davis said. "And I'm still learning the ropes. I always will be. But I will say this." He paused, his fingers clutching hers. "Marriage is truly a sacred trust. You hold each other's hearts in your hands. Be kind, be humble, be patient. And listen."

22

Bridget

Careful not to wake Sean, Bridget slipped out of bed as dawn was touching the lake. She stood by the veranda doors and watched the sun brighten the day, then slipped into jeans and a T-shirt. Charlotte's mention of how early she rose had sparked an idea.

She was going to bring her darling husband breakfast in bed. After cramming her feet into sneakers without socks, she slipped out the door into the silent hallway. Holding her breath, she pulled the door shut and released the knob.

On the way downstairs, she paused to check the view from various windows, her writer's mind storing notes for her book. While using too many descriptive details was frowned upon in novels nowadays, judicious, perfect little details could bring a story to life. That's what Bridget strove for, a vibrant, rich tale that would immerse her readers.

Humming and the clanging of pots announced that Charlotte was already hard at work in the kitchen. Bridget paused in the doorway, waiting for her hostess to notice her. "Good morning," Charlotte said with a broad smile. "Sleep well?"

Bridget nodded. "I sure did. Our room is so comfortable."

"Help yourself to coffee." Charlotte pointed to the station. "Just made a fresh pot."

"I will, thanks." Bridget took a tentative step into the room. "I was wondering, can I take breakfast on a tray upstairs? I want to surprise Sean."

Charlotte smiled indulgently. "Of course. This morning I'm making omelets, if he likes those. With fresh crabmeat or bacon. Veggies, cheese, whatever people want."

Bridget's belly contracted with hunger. "Wow, crabmeat omelets sound fantastic. I don't think I've ever had one."

Charlotte laughed. "Then you haven't lived. The classic style includes asparagus and hollandaise sauce. Want that?"

"Definitely." Feeling more comfortable about entering the cook's domain, Bridget crossed to the coffee area and poured a cup. After adding cream, she perched on a stool at the island to watch Charlotte work.

After a couple of minutes, she said, "We loved the strawberry barbecue sauce. I hope you win the contest."

The chef smiled. "I'm glad you enjoyed it. That's my real goal, to make people happy." She briskly whisked a bowl of eggs. "A lot of my dishes are simple, especially in my cookbooks, so people can make them at home."

Bridget groaned. "That's good. I hate it when I read a recipe and there's some fancy ingredient I don't have."

"I hear you. Some chefs are more about making a statement." Charlotte turned her attention to the asparagus she was steaming. "What are you and Sean doing today?"

Tea at Julep's. Although the upcoming meeting was never far from her thoughts, this concrete reminder sent a jolt through Bridget. Maybe today she would learn something concrete about her parentage.

Or not. Discouragement swept over her.

Realizing that she hadn't answered Charlotte, she said, "Oh, we're having tea with a local historian. Julep Buckley."

"Julep? Oh yes, she's an expert on local history." Charlotte pulled the asparagus pot off the burner, then gave the hollandaise sauce a stir. "This for your book?"

Bridget squirmed on the stool. She'd confided in Grace so not telling

Charlotte the truth felt rude. "I'm researching my family history," she said, thinking her life story was a bit much to go into at the moment. "I think they may have come from around here."

Charlotte's eyes lit up. "Really? What were their names?"

Her hand went to her locket. "I don't know." *Beyond Lula, that is.* She forced a smile. "I was adopted."

"Oh, Bridget." Those crystal-blue eyes filled with sympathy. "I had no idea."

Bridget shrugged. "No big deal, really. I had wonderful adoptive parents. But sometimes I want to know more." She picked up her mug. "Medical reasons, at the very least."

"I can understand that." Charlotte tasted the sauce, then nodded. "Good luck. I hope Julep can help."

"Me too." Julep had seemed to recognize the locket so hopefully she'd have some substantial information. If she didn't, Bridget didn't know what she'd do. She had the registry, but that depended upon waiting for her birth mother or father to respond.

What if they never did? She mentally shook her head. If they didn't, she'd be no worse off than she was now. And her life was pretty fantastic, actually. Right now, for example, when she was just about to take a scrumptious breakfast to her loving husband.

"I'm no chef but I'm good at making toast," Bridget said. "Let me know if I can help."

"Okay. Take your choice of bread." Charlotte tipped her chin toward the bread keeper, which held a variety of loaves.

Bridget chose a white sourdough loaf she remembered from previous breakfasts and loaded the four-slot toaster. Soon the appetizing aroma of toasting bread joined that drifting from the stove, where Charlotte was preparing the omelets. Sunshine streamed through the windows, glinting off polished stainless steel, glass, and granite counters, making the kitchen a cheerful place to be on such a lovely morning. Beyond an open window over the sink, birds chirped as they rustled in the bushes.

Bridget was happy, she realized as she peeked at the browning toast. Taking a trip to Magnolia Harbor had been a great decision. Her heart beat slightly faster in anticipation. And now she had her husband here to share it with.

Grace entered the kitchen, dressed in jeans and a T-shirt. She crossed to the coffee station. "Good morning." She smiled at Bridget. "Did you sleep well?"

"We sure did, thanks," Bridget said. The toast popped and she pulled it out onto the breadboard and began to butter the slices. "I'm taking Sean breakfast in bed."

"What a nice thought." Grace poured cream into her coffee. Turning to Charlotte, she said, "I keep forgetting. We need to go on our shopping trip." At Charlotte's puzzled expression, she said, "For the dinner dance the last night of the festival?"

"Oh, yeah." Charlotte smoothed her hands on her apron. "I've been so busy thinking about the contest I forgot. Yes, let's go. Miss Millie's has some cute dresses."

Bridget had window-shopped at Miss Millie's downtown. Despite the old-fashioned name, the boutique stocked up-to-date styles. "I love that store."

"Are you staying for the dance, Bridget?" Grace asked, a finger on her lips. She nodded. "That's right, you'll be here. Why don't you come with us tomorrow? Girls' day out."

"I'd love to." Bridget felt a rush of pleasure. Now that Sean was here, she had a reason to dress up for the dance.

"Maybe Anne will come along too," Charlotte said.

Grace took a sip of coffee. "Sounds like a plan." Carrying the cup, she walked toward the doorway. "I'll go check the dining room."

Bridget arrived upstairs a few minutes later, struggling a bit with the unwieldy breakfast tray. Somehow she managed to open the door, close it behind her with a bump of her hip, and set the tray down on the table.

"What's all this?" Sean asked, pushing himself to a seated position. "Breakfast in bed?"

Bridget grabbed a napkin and mopped up a small coffee spill. "That's right, milord. Crabmeat omelet, sourdough toast, and Charlotte's famous home fries." She carried a mug to him, holding a napkin underneath. "And coffee and juice of course."

Sean surveyed the pristine white bed linens and laughed. "I think we'd better eat out on the veranda. You know what a slob I am."

Bridget considered his point. There was a small table on the veranda they could use. "Okay, let's do that." She opened the French door and ferried the tray outside. Sean jumped out of bed and washed up, then joined her, wearing a T-shirt and shorts.

They dug into the meal, not talking for a few minutes. Then Sean asked, "Tell me about your book."

Prickles of pleasure washed over Bridget. Although Sean didn't read romances as a rule, he was her biggest fan—and a great person to brainstorm ideas with. "Okay. This is what I have so far." She set down her fork. "Annabelle is an orphan who lives with her aunt and uncle in a house much like this one."

Sean raised a brow. "An orphan?"

His repeat of her words sparked a realization in Bridget. Annabelle's situation held elements of her life, even if in a subtle way. "Huh. I guess I've been thinking about my adoption a lot." *Constantly.* "Yeah, so Annabelle is loved, but of course she misses her parents. She's also new to town"—another commonality—"so she sees my fictional Magnolia Harbor with curious eyes."

"Good way to keep it fresh." Sean crunched a piece of toast.

"Thanks, hon. I try." In her writing, Bridget had found that a character new to a setting could see and react strongly to a place. Much like the reader, hopefully, who was also unfamiliar with it.

"So who's the love interest?" Sean's eyes sparkled with mischief. He liked to pretend that she modeled the handsome hunks in her stories after him. Actually, he wasn't far wrong. Thanks to their early relationship, Bridget was able to conjure up the turbulent and exciting feelings of falling in love.

Very handy for a romance author.

Bridget nibbled on her omelet, the flavors of melted cheese and crabmeat flooding her taste buds. "That's still shaping up. I was thinking that her aunt and uncle want her to marry a banker, but she's got her eyes on a mechanic. A tinkerer on horseless carriages, which of course were new then. He races them too. I've moved the date to 1902. Greenville held an event that included an automobile race that year." After coming across that tidbit of history, she'd incorporated it into her novel.

"Aha. Kind of like me." Sean was in the middle of rebuilding a souped-up GTO, his dream car as a young man.

She regarded her husband with narrowed eyes, his curls burnished by the morning light. "I *was* thinking of making him a redhead, although that is rare in romantic fiction." Most heroes were either dark and brooding or blond and chiseled.

Sean laughed. "Except that Scottish guy in that popular time-travel book and television show. There are lots of Scots in the South, remember."

"I did know that, thanks." After the Battle of Culloden, many Scots had emigrated to North and South Carolina. Bridget mused over his suggestion. She'd give her hero a Scottish surname, she decided. Something relatable but not overly common. Oh, Macintosh. *His nickname could be Tosh . . .*

"I've lost you," Sean teased. "Back in book world?"

Bridget shook her thoughts away and focused on her husband. "Sorry." Out on the lake, two kayaks moved in tandem, a man and a woman energetically plying the long paddles. "Want to go out on the lake this morning? There are kayaks we can borrow."

Sean craned his neck to watch the kayakers. "I have an idea. Let's paddle over to town and look around the festival. It's not too far." He smiled. "I promised Molly we'd buy her something."

"I'll bet." Molly had her father wrapped around her little finger. "I saw some cute things when I was over there the other day. So sure, let's do that." Maybe the lively scene would distract her from thinking about the impending meeting with Julep.

A couple of hours later at the festival, Bridget was leafing through embellished T-shirts when Presley came strolling along. The nurse was dressed in jeans and a gauzy top, and cute gold sandals adorned her feet. But she looked tired, Bridget noticed, especially when she lifted her sunglasses and revealed circles under her eyes. No wonder, after that scene at the inn the previous evening. Not only had Presley been upset, Curt had seemed to be devastated.

"Hey, Bridget," Presley said. "Enjoying the festival?"

"I am." Bridget looked over at Sean, who was sorting through old vinyl records at an adjacent booth. "My husband is in seventh heaven over there."

Presley swiveled to look. "Oh, I didn't know he was here with you."

"He wasn't, until yesterday." Bridget felt her lips curve in a smile. "He flew down and surprised me."

The nurse crossed her arms across her midriff. "How romantic." Her words were light but Bridget detected a note of sadness underneath. While Bridget continued to look through the shirts, trying to decide between pale pink and aqua, the other woman stood without speaking.

"Have you ever overreacted and regretted it later?" Presley asked.

"All the time." Bridget tried to soften the heavy conversation with a little laugh. "Don't even get Sean started."

Presley blew air out with a huff. "I don't know what came over me. I thought things were going well with Curt but when he pulled out a ring . . . well, I kind of flipped out."

Bridget kept her eyes on the shirts to give the other woman a little space. Presley must be desperate if she was confiding in someone she barely knew. But she could relate all too well, having experienced her own turmoil as a younger woman. Tangled emotions could sweep over you like storms, leading to arguments and misunderstandings. But was Presley's reaction due to a general aversion toward the idea of marrying Curt or something else?

"You weren't expecting it, huh?" Bridget said.

Presley rolled her eyes. "No. We were engaged years ago and broke up, mainly because Curt was too self-centered. That doctor ego thing, you know?"

Bridget glanced at Presley. "So he's still that way?"

Presley bit her lip, confusion shadowing her eyes. "No, actually he's not. He seems to have changed. But then he pops the question after what, a week?"

"You need more time." It wasn't a question.

"Yes. Yes, I do." Presley's face lit up, then fell. "But I wonder if he'll even talk to me after I humiliated him that way."

Bridget decided upon the pink shirt and put the aqua one back on the rack. "Oh, I think he will. He must really love you. And love covers a multitude of sins."

The hope in Presley's eyes hurt Bridget's heart. "You think?"

Sean was walking toward Bridget, a huge grin on his face. He was clutching six albums under his arm.

"I *know*," Bridget said simply. "Go find him and tell him you love him too."

Presley's hand went to her lips, a faraway expression on her pretty features. Then she whirled around and trotted off, determination squaring her slender shoulders.

"What was all that about?" Sean asked, staring after Presley with a furrowed brow.

"Don't ask," Bridget said. She held up the pink shirt, the sequins decorating it glinting in the sunshine. "What do you think? Will Molly like it?"

On the dot of three o'clock, she and Sean strolled up Julep's front path, which was edged with flowering azaleas. As they drew closer, Bridget saw a screened-in porch to one side, and there the historian sat, waiting.

"Come around on the lawn, honey," she called, waving her hand.

Clutching Sean's arm, Bridget steered them onto a side path that wound around to the porch. Bees buzzed among clumps of jasmine and mock orange. Blooming dogwoods set among taller trees gave an enchanted effect of floating blossoms.

Before they climbed the brick steps to the porch, Bridget paused to drink it all in. Maybe she'd have Annabelle's best friend live here, in this brick Colonial-style house. What a wonderful setting. Then her heart gave a lurch and began to pound as she recalled the real reason they were here. Could Julep help Bridget find her mother? In a daze, she barely noticed as Sean pushed open the screen door and held it to let her enter.

"Who do we have here?" Julep extended a tiny hand, smiling up at Sean.

"This is my husband, Sean. He surprised me with a visit from Boston, where we live." Bridget's cheeks felt stiff when she smiled. Hopefully the courtesies and chitchat would be brief.

"Nice to meet you, Sean." Julep motioned toward a wicker sofa. "Please have a seat." Their hostess returned to her own wicker chair. "Sweet tea? Or would you prefer unsweetened?"

Bridget was touched. Julep had made two pitchers of tea, probably figuring that Northerners might not care for tea with so much added sugar.

Sean glanced at her for a clue. "I'll take sweet tea, Julep," Bridget said. "I've become fond of it while staying at the inn."

"Me too," her husband hastily added. He pulled out a handkerchief and dabbed at his forehead. "It will be refreshing on such a hot day."

"And it's only May," Julep said as she poured tea, the ice tinkling. "But of course three o'clock is the warmest time of the day."

Bridget had noticed the heat intensified over the course of the day here, rather than reaching its peak at noon, as seemed to happen in New England.

They sipped quietly for a few moments, Sean accepting a lemon cookie from an offered plate. They watched the birds flitting around feeders in the garden. At one point, Julep picked up a pad and pencil and made a notation. "I keep a list of my feathered visitors," she said. "I've seen some rare birds but I love them all, even the common sparrows."

"My mom does that too," Sean offered. "She was pretty excited when she saw an eagle in our yard one day."

While Julep and Sean talked about birds, Bridget sat clutching her locket and sipping her tea mindlessly.

"Bridget, dear, you're here in Magnolia Harbor to research your family?"

Finally. Bridget started to speak, then had to clear her throat. "That's right. I was adopted, you see, and I have reason to believe I was born here. Well, in South Carolina, anyway."

Julep pursed her lips, her eyes raking every detail of Bridget's face. "Interesting. May I ask what led you here?"

"Not much, really." Bridget laughed. Her quest was so hopeless, wasn't it? Like finding a needle in a haystack. "My adoptive mother mentioned this town. And she gave me this." Bridget held out the locket, then dropped it and fumbled with the clasp. "This was given to my parents when they got me."

Julep took the locket and examined it closely with curious eyes, even opening it, although nothing was inside.

Bridget scooted forward on the sofa. "See how it says *Lula*? I saw a locket just like it in a portrait at the Jackson House Museum. Olympia Jackson was wearing it."

The historian held up the chain, allowing the locket to swing and catch the light. "The Jacksons had a tradition of passing down the locket," she said. "If this is the same one . . ."

"It has to be," Bridget blurted. "How many lockets with *Lula* on them do you suppose there are? And there's the mention of Magnolia Harbor too, don't forget." She sank back, chagrined at her outburst. "I'm sorry. The whole thing's been weighing on my mind. So frustrating."

"I can understand that," Julep said. "But I'm not sure how or why you had this." She swung it again. "Olympia did have a daughter, her only child—"

"Could *she* be my mother?" Bridget winced as she heard her voice rise again.

Julep studied her for a long moment, sympathy in her eyes. "I really don't know, dear. Tallulah Jackson left town decades ago. And no one has seen or heard from her since."

23

Anne

The shade was deep and cool under the arbor, which was covered in gorgeous wisteria vines. The almost cloying scent of the hanging purple flowers filled the air, attracting swarms of bees.

Anne sat back in the wicker chair with a sigh. She'd rarely felt so at peace. Even as a child, her moments of happiness were soon tainted by yet another confrontation with her mother. She had one specific memory, of gazing up into a clear blue sky and experiencing a surge of pure joy. She'd been in love, and the world was beautiful.

Then she'd gone into the house and her mother had brushed off her excited confidences then berated her about the state of her room, bringing Anne down to earth with a painful crash. She had even emptied the bureau drawers on the bed so Anne could redo the contents. Her folding was never good enough. Anne was more of a stuffer—still was, sad to say.

Davis couldn't care less. She loved that about him, the way he accepted her, flaws and all. She thought back to his words to Curt the previous night. *Sacred trust . . . kind . . . humble . . . listen.* She laughed out loud. He was a gem, there was no other word for it.

Mother was bitter and miserable. She couldn't stand to see me happy, either. The realization sank into her mind, certainty growing as she considered this insight. Anne had always thought she was the source of her mother's distress, that if she, Anne, were only perfect, her mother would finally love her.

Anne tipped her head to stare at the sky, blue as that long-ago day. Deep, endless, gorgeous. Again she felt that bright, buoyant joy. Davis loved her. And she loved him. That was what mattered now.

Davis came into view, picking his way along the lawn while carrying two tall glasses. The dear man was bringing her iced tea.

They'd had a lazy day, hanging around the inn for the most part, although Davis had slipped out to play a few holes of golf. Anne had welcomed the downtime, the lack of any requirement except to lounge. And eat. Charlotte Wilde was an incredible chef. Although the inn didn't usually serve lunch, she'd made them a chicken and grape salad with pecans that was to die for. Even sweeter, Charlotte and Grace had invited her to go dress shopping the next day. She hadn't gone on a girls' day out for ages.

"You can play golf all day tomorrow," she told Davis as he handed her a frosty glass. The cubes tinkled as she lifted it to her mouth.

"What's this?" Davis settled himself in the adjacent wicker chair, which creaked slightly. He chuckled. "Trying to get rid of me?"

"No, silly. I'm going shopping with the girls. So I thought you'd like to play golf while we're gone."

"Aha. An all-day shopping event. Should I worry?" Rolling his eyes in mock horror, he clutched at his back pocket, where he carried his wallet.

Anne laughed. "I'll just buy one dress, promise. For the dance."

His brows went up. "Oh, the dance. I heard something about that."

She leaned toward him. "You're not getting out of it this time, mister." She and Davis had a running joke about his supposed lack of dancing ability. He was actually quite good, once she could drag him out onto the floor.

"You'll owe me, big time." That was another of their jokes. Usually Anne paid the debt by allowing him an extra golf day without complaint.

Anne smiled. "It's a deal." She drained the rest of her tea with a rattle of cubes. "Now how about going for a ride? I'll drive."

For once, Davis, who preferred to be at the wheel, didn't protest. "Taking me sightseeing, Annie? Lead on."

Anne's palms were slick on the wheel. Not only did she rarely drive the SUV, she had a knot in her stomach the size of a boulder. As she drove along Lake Haven Road, she thought more than once about turning around and heading back to the inn.

But now that she'd started to reveal her lifelong secrets to Davis, she found she couldn't stop. Even if she was telling the whole sad story one snippet at a time. Anne laughed to herself. Maybe she should ask Bridget how to do that, since she was an author.

Anne signaled and turned down a side road, noticing the new buildings on both sides. As they drove past, she saw they were doctors' offices. She remembered a time when there were only two or three doctors in town, family physicians who took care of patients from birth to grave.

No doubt Magnolia Harbor was growing, the way many South Carolina towns were. Not only was there an influx of retirees, but young families and corporations alike had come to seek new opportunity. And being near the coast, on a huge lake, must mean this area was very desirable.

"You're taking me to the hospital?" Davis read the huge sign beside the entrance road. "Going to lock me up?"

"It's not that kind of hospital," Anne said with a laugh. She slowed as she reached the front, then turned into the closest visitor lot. The three-story brick structure looked the same, with maybe an addition or two at the back. "This is where I was born." She figured she might as well start with something easy, as a warm-up to the difficult stuff.

Davis peered out at the building. "Hmm. Interesting." His tone said otherwise, although he was being polite. "Similar to the one where Cora had me." No doubt that was true, since this building was typical of many of the same vintage.

Only a few people were crossing the parking lot toward the main entrance. With a start, Anne recognized Curt, who was carrying a big bouquet of roses. She groaned.

Davis turned his head and saw Curt. He waved but, intent on reaching the door, the young doctor didn't see him. "I wonder what he's up to. Visiting someone?"

Anne shook her head. "Yes, his former fiancée, Presley, I'm sure." Hopefully the nurse wouldn't take a personal delivery of flowers the wrong way. She'd been quite blunt in her treatment of Curt the night before.

"Oh, Presley. Nice young woman. I hope it works out for him."

Anne put the SUV in gear. "On to the next place." The knot in her belly tightened. She hadn't been to their next destination in four decades. It had been a warm spring day exactly like this, the beautiful weather a mockery of her grief. Hopefully she'd be able to maintain her composure.

The route took them out of Magnolia Harbor, to a neighboring village. Davis glanced around curiously. "Snellville? Did you live here too?"

"I didn't," Anne said. "But someone I was . . . very close to did." She slowed as they traveled along the narrow main street, gracious homes in lush gardens on either side. Snellville was a working-class town but it was pretty and charming, despite lacking the tourist dollars Magnolia Harbor enjoyed.

They reached the crossroads at the center of town, marked by a blinking light. Anne turned left, onto a road that led deeper into the countryside. Another couple of miles and they were there, at the white Baptist church nestled under tall pines.

This time of day, the parking lot was empty, and Anne was glad. She remembered the people being nice and kind but she didn't really want to talk to anyone. Or explain where she'd been ever since that day. She'd never returned, not once.

Her palms moistened as she put the car in park and turned off the engine. "We're walking from here," she told her husband.

He gave her a quizzical look but didn't argue. After they crunched across the gravel and reached a gate set between two wide oaks, a look of understanding crossed his face. "Oh, is your mother buried here?" The sign arching over the gate read, *Shady Rest Cemetery.*

"Not my mother," Anne said. As they strolled along the grassy paths, her breath came in pants. Her vision narrowed to the route ahead, to the simple stone that lay in a far corner, past that tall angel bending over a family plot.

"Anne, are you all right?" Davis's face loomed close. He put a hand on her arm. "You're all clammy."

She stopped moving and bowed her head, staring down toward her feet. A few violets spangled the grass, she noticed, and she focused on them, taking in every detail.

"Do you need to sit down?" Davis asked, his breath tickling her ear. He put an arm around her. "We don't need to do this, you know. Not if it's going to make you ill."

Anne swallowed hard and gritted her teeth. "No, I need to." She shuffled her sneakers forward and he dropped his arm.

Step by step, she advanced across the cemetery. A light breeze tossed the trees, where singing birds sat. She remembered the mausoleum set into a slope, the iron doors long locked, the date *1922* engraved in brass above the door. Only a few more feet . . .

And they were there, at the Matherly plot.

A hundred years ago, someone had installed a decorative iron fence to mark the plot's boundaries. Sections leaned this way and that, the metal corroded by the air, salt-laden even this far inland. Dry leaves from the previous autumn littered the enclosure, evidence that not many visitors came this way.

Anne's eyes rested on a more recent stone, the carving clear and sharp. She swallowed again but this time her throat was too dry, so an awkward choking sound came out. She felt her husband staring at her but he didn't speak.

Finally she was able to whisper, "That's Beau Matherly's grave." She sank down onto the grass. "He was my fiancé."

24

Bridget

Bridget barely listened to Sean and Julep as they chatted about Strawberry Fest. Her brain kept repeating Julep's words over and over: *No one has seen or heard from her since.* Tallulah Jackson had vanished. She could be anywhere. She could be dead. There wasn't any way to find out if she was Bridget's birth mother. And without more information, even Julep, with her encyclopedic knowledge, couldn't help her.

An idea flashed into her mind. Maybe Presley could help. The hospital must keep records of births. If she found out that a girl was born on Bridget's birthday, maybe that would further confirm that she was from Magnolia Harbor. Where she would go from there, she had no idea.

Was there a special prayer for people at a dead end? If so, she needed it.

Presley had given her a cell phone number during their first meeting so Bridget sent off a quick text. The nurse wrote back right away and said that, yes, she would check the records, but she wouldn't be able to reveal any identifying information—she would only be able to answer yes or no. Blessedly, she didn't ask why Bridget was inquiring.

Her hand went to the locket, the clue that promised much but delivered nothing. Her mother could have found it. Bought it in a pawn shop or secondhand shop. Or even stolen it.

Ha. She wasn't going to go that far, to believe that her mother was a petty thief.

"Ready, Bridget?" Sean asked, placing a hand on her knee.

She awoke from her thoughts. "Yes." She stood, smiling at Julep. "Thanks for the tea and your help. I might be back if I learn something new."

The older woman's eyes were kind. "Please feel free to call or visit any time. You've quite stirred up my curiosity with this mystery."

"Mine too," Bridget said with a wry grimace. "I guess I thought it would be easy." After all, she often had wonderful success while researching her books. Her inquisitive, talented nose helped her ferret out the most interesting and relevant snippets of information.

Julep patted her shoulder. "Nothing worthwhile is ever easy." She laughed. "Now there's a cliché I resent."

Bridget and Sean joined in. "Me too," Bridget said fervently. "Anyway, we'll be here a couple more days so hopefully we'll see you again."

"I hope so too," Julep called after them, standing on the steps while they descended into the garden. "I'll be at the dance, with bells on."

Halfway back to the street, Bridget felt tears burn her eyes. "Oh, Sean. I'm so disappointed." She slipped her arm through his, leaning on his warm, strong shoulder. "I guess I thought she'd say I was Tallulah's long-lost daughter."

"That would have been nice," Sean said. "But don't give up yet, honey. You still might be."

A spark of hope lit in Bridget's heart. "Want to go to the Jackson House Museum? I think it's still open. You can see my locket in the portrait of Olympia."

The museum *was* still open, and so was the library Bridget saw as they drove past. They had evening hours, which meant she and Sean could go there next.

"Good afternoon." The same docent greeted them.

Becky, that was her name. "Hi, Becky," Bridget said. "This is my husband, Sean. We're going to take a peek around." She handed the docent the fee.

"Take your time." The docent opened a metal box and stashed the bills. "We're slow today, due to the festival. There's a popular band playing at the bandstand right now. And the strawberry pie eating contest is going on."

"Which one draws the most spectators, I wonder?" Sean joked. "Even I can't imagine eating a whole pie. Ouch."

"They gobble 'em down like truffle-seeking hogs," Becky said. "It's quite a sight."

Smiling at the picture the docent's words created, Bridget took the tickets and tucked them into her pocket. "We won't be too long. I want to stop by the library after."

Becky's eyes widened. "They're open until eight o'clock tonight." She shook her head. "You two really are different than most. Museum and library instead of pie-eating and banjo-picking."

"Oh, we'll probably take those in too," Sean said with his friendly grin. "Is there anything in particular you recommend us taking a peek at?"

"There's too much to list." Becky snatched up a brochure and opened it to Sean's view. "This house is stuffed full of treasures. You can enter every room with an open door." She gave him a rundown.

Bridget listened with half an ear, more interested in absorbing the serene, elegant atmosphere of the place. Had her mother actually lived here? The mansion was worlds away from the modest but comfortable split-level her adoptive parents owned. Despite her vivid imagination, she couldn't quite picture real people living here, not modern-day ones anyway.

"By the way," Bridget told the docent before they set off, "I did learn something about the family." She pointed at the portrait. "Olympia had a daughter, Tallulah, but no one is sure where she is." She swallowed. "Or if she's even alive."

Becky narrowed her eyes in speculation. "Interesting. Thanks for that. Maybe the committee can find out more."

Maybe the committee already knows, Bridget thought, *and was keeping the family's sad history quiet*. But she merely nodded. "See you back here in a while."

First Bridget and Sean stopped to study the portrait from the closest vantage point, the staircase. "See how it's identical." Bridget held out her locket, speaking in a whisper so Becky wouldn't overhear.

Sean glanced back and forth between the painting and Bridget's necklace. "Sure looks that way. Think Lula is a nickname for Tallulah?"

Bridget tucked the necklace back inside her shirt. "That's a strong possibility."

"I agree." Sean nodded. "Shall we go up?"

They trudged up the elaborate staircase, pausing now and then to take in the view through strategically placed windows or interior details of the home's fine construction. Wood gleamed everywhere, set off by flocked wallpaper and acres of Persian carpet.

Several doors lined the upper hall, but only two of them stood open. Mindful of Becky's instructions, they only went into those rooms. The first was large, with a four-poster bed draped with yellow silk. Curtains at the windows were made of the same fabric, and figures in the carpet echoed the theme of jasmine blossoms and birds in the paintings and figurines placed on surfaces throughout the room. The furniture was polished mahogany that gleamed in the filtered light.

"Wow," Sean breathed. "This is magnificent."

Bridget agreed, but her attention was focused on the nightstand, where a silver photograph frame stood. She shuffled across the carpet to take a closer look. Sean was reading the plaque aloud, which informed them the furniture was made in the 1700s by Southern craftsmen. The frame wasn't that old, but it was vintage, discolored by tarnish. In this humidity, keeping silver clean must be a real challenge.

Bridget wasn't sure what she was expecting, but it wasn't a photograph of an older woman frowning into the camera. She quickly recognized Olympia from the portrait, her hair turned gray and piled up in an updo. The high-necked blouse she wore made her resemble a strict schoolmarm.

Was the photograph an indication of a large ego? After all, who kept a picture of themselves beside their bed? She bit her lip, realizing she was being uncharitable. Maybe the museum staff had placed the picture there, to indicate this was Olympia's bedroom. She settled the frame into place with a soft grunt of disappointment.

"What do you have there?" Sean asked. He came over to study the photograph. "Is that Olympia? She looks like a mean old lady."

Bridget elbowed him, both chagrined and amused, although she'd never admit to the latter. "Cut it out. She was probably miserable. Remember, her daughter took off? Think how we'd feel if Molly did that." Her words cast a chill over the room as both parents pondered that horrible idea.

"Let's finish looking around here," Sean said. "Then maybe we can learn more about the Jacksons at the library."

The other bedroom available for public viewing had deep window seats overlooking the rear gardens. Had Tallulah sat in those seats, daydreaming about her future? Bridget could picture a teenager doing that. She went to the window and perched on the painted wood, leaning gently against the glass to look out. Where her hand rested, there was something uneven under the paint.

She peered more closely, making out a faint etching: the letter T and a plus sign. So this might well have been Tallulah's room, then.

Bridget couldn't read the second letter, since a zealous sanding job had obscured it. She rubbed her fingers over the lettering. What other secrets had been covered up by time? Or scoured from this house?

At the library, their next stop, the seemingly tireless Phyllis was working behind the desk, checking in a huge stack of books. She smiled as they entered. "Nice to see you again, Bridget." Her bright gaze went beyond Bridget to Sean.

Bridget bit back amusement and introduced Sean. "We're going to do some more research in the local history room."

Phyllis nodded in that direction. "Go on ahead. You're an expert by now." As the pair walked that way, she called, "Hasn't gotten so much use in years." A peal of laughter followed those words.

"I get the feeling these ladies are glad you're around," Sean commented as Bridget flicked on the light switch. "They seem happy to share their knowledge with someone."

"I find that's true pretty much everywhere I do research." Bridget went to the file cabinet to choose rolls of microfilm. Now that she had a name, she planned to scour local newspapers for mention of Tallulah Jackson. Hopefully pictures would be included.

They found a photo of Tallulah holding one end of a big check, surrounded by other girls with long hair and short dresses. It had been the early 1970s, after all. "Junior League teens raise money for children's program," read the caption. Tallulah's hair, worn in a flip, was dark, like Bridget's, but she was petite in stature, with very different features.

"She doesn't look like me at all," Bridget said. She could hear the disappointment in her own voice.

Sean, peering over her shoulder, said, "Maybe you look like your father. Molly takes after my side, remember." Molly resembled her aunt, Sean's sister, leggy and redheaded, with adorable freckles.

"You're right about that." Bridget stared at the grainy photograph, searing Tallulah's features into her brain. Was this pretty young woman her mother? Or was she totally on the wrong track?

Sean had wandered to the shelves. "Hey, they have yearbooks here. Let's take a peek." He bent and pulled out several for the relevant years.

They sat together and leafed through the books. "Yearbooks from any year, any place, look the same," Sean commented. He was right. The sports teams, the goofy candid photographs, the beauties, brains, and jocks. Only the hairstyles and fashions changed.

Tallulah had been a leader, Bridget thought. She was on several sports teams and acted in plays. One prom photograph showed her in the arms of a much taller boy, Tallulah making a face at the camera. She squinted at the boy, but only the curve of his cheek was visible as he smiled at his date. He had broad shoulders and big hands, she could see that much.

Is that my father? Or was it merely one dance out of many that Tallulah had enjoyed?

Sean made a noise. When she looked over, he held up the yearbook. "Tallulah didn't graduate," he said. "See? This is where her picture should have gone." He showed her where, alphabetically, Tallulah should appear.

Bridget was born in October. By June her mother would have been several months pregnant. In those days, she knew, pregnant students often withdrew or were expelled. Not being allowed to graduate? No doubt par for the course, unfortunately.

It fit. Maybe Tallulah *was* her mother. But where was she now?

Anne

A rustling sound told Anne that Davis was sitting beside her on the grass. Although he didn't say anything, she could sense his shock. She'd never mentioned Beau to him, not really. She'd said something about a high school sweetheart that hadn't worked out.

That was an understatement if she'd ever heard one.

Finally, Davis spoke. "Tell me about him, Anne. I see he was only eighteen when he passed."

Eighteen. She was more than three times that age now. Poor Beau. He never had the chance to get married, have children, grow older with a loved one. Experience all the joys and sorrows of adulthood.

"He was in the service. It was a training accident. The helicopter he was riding in went down." She hadn't been there of course, but the imagined scene was seared into her mind. As she had then, she wrenched her mind away.

"Anne." His hand tightened over hers. "I'm so sorry." The anguish in his voice told her he was sincere.

She blinked back tears, her grief mingling with gratitude. Davis had such a big heart, such true compassion. Many men wouldn't care if a previous rival for her affections had died. After all, she would be married to Beau if he'd lived, right? But not Davis. Now, as always, his concern was for her.

Anne leaned against his shoulder with hers. "Thanks, Davis." Her voice was husky. "My mother never approved of Beau but he was a good boy. He came from a poor family, on the wrong side of the tracks." She snorted. "What a cliché, but she actually said that. Going into the service was the only way he could think to improve himself." A knife of sorrow sliced her already tender heart into ribbons. "He was so smart. And talented too. Could fix anything broken you put in front of him."

Images flashed into her mind. The big grin that glowed like sunrise across his freckled face. His silky dark hair, which had a habit of falling into his equally dark eyes. The way his handsome features formed an earnest expression whenever he was thinking hard or working on something. He'd always carried a ballpoint pen and paper to jot down his ideas and thoughts. He'd planned to further his schooling after finishing his stint in the military.

A sob burst out of Anne. Poor, poor Beau. He had been taken too soon, had never reached his potential. No doubt he was a big hit in heaven, though. She could picture that too, she found, Beau whole and happy, having a good time hanging out with all the other saints.

These thoughts made her chuckle, earning a confused glance from her husband. She squeezed his hand and explained. "You probably think I'm nuts," she said.

"Not at all," he said slowly. "You'll see Beau again someday, Anne. I know it."

A bird chirping in a nearby bush underscored the graveyard's quiet serenity. Davis was right, but for now, no matter how much she missed Beau, he was out of reach.

That's why, despite assurances of future reunions, it was important to let people know you loved them. She kissed Davis, a quick peck on the lips. "You've always meant the world to me, you know that? How did I get so lucky?" After Beau's death, Anne had thought she'd never find love again. But she had, and although different than that potent first romance, her relationship with Davis was deep and solid and real. Something she could build a life upon. And had. But even the best foundation could be improved. Strengthened. A thought drifted into her mind, a notion carrying the weight of a command. She acknowledged its authority. *Yes.*

"I'm the lucky one," Davis was murmuring. "Ever since I saw you that day . . ." He moved closer for another kiss.

She kissed him. "I have one more thing to show you, Davis." Her belly hollowed at hearing her own words. Was she ready? No, not really. But it was time. She'd learned to trust that small, still voice.

His face blanched a little but he didn't protest. "Lead on." He unfolded his legs and stood, then reached out a hand to help her rise.

Thankful for the leverage, Anne pushed herself into a standing position, groaning softly due to creaky knees. She didn't do much sitting on the ground these days. She brushed off the rear of her capri pants and led the way back to their car.

"Let's stop and get cold drinks," she suggested. "It's a bit of a ride."

Just up the road, they found an old country store. The weathered clapboards still held traces of faded signs and the standing Pegasus gas sign promised fuel no longer offered. But inside, the moisture-beaded coolers were stocked with soft drinks and the shelves crammed with goods ranging from local vegetables to bags of candy. Davis grabbed a couple of colas and the packaged cakes they'd both devoured in childhood. He gave Anne a crooked smile. "Perfect fare for a trip down memory lane."

Anne nodded in agreement although her stomach was too knotted to eat anything, even chocolate and marshmallow. The cola, though, was perfect, sweet and icy goodness.

"Where are we going?" Davis asked a few minutes later, as Anne turned onto the highway ramp.

"Charleston." Anne loved the old city, perhaps the most gracious, gorgeous town in the South. But underneath the memories of good times, great food and shopping sprees, lay something darker, a place she had walled off like . . . like that mausoleum at Shady Rest. A good analogy, she told herself. Dead, buried, and locked away.

Now she was opening the door, turning the key in a rusty, resistant lock. Would she be able to withstand what she found? Would Davis?

They would have to. Sometimes there was no choice. "Get on with it," had been one of her mother's favorite sayings. What was it with that older generation, so stoic and dutiful, often at great expense? Anne had hated hearing that phrase, which seemed to negate her feelings, doubts, and objections, as if they didn't matter. Didn't exist. But maybe in this case her mother was right.

Once they reached the city proper, Anne had to stop and consult her phone for directions. Not only had Charleston grown and changed, she'd forgotten the route. Sometimes refusing to think about something actually worked. She'd certainly done a good job in this case.

Davis waited patiently while she figured things out, which was unusual. Normally he would have questioned her, made suggestions, even taken over. She'd learned to see this somewhat annoying habit as proof of a protective, helpful nature.

"I see where I went wrong," she said, after zooming in on the map. "I should have turned left at the last intersection, not right."

After some maneuvering, Anne got them turned around and going in the right direction. This time she turned down the correct side street and soon found the cul-de-sac that was her destination.

The house looked the same—sprawling and white, with multiple wings. The same hundred-year oaks towered over the grounds, providing shade, and neat boxwood hedges still guarded the frontage. A discreet, small sign was still on the brick gatepost.

"What is this place?" Davis asked after Anne parked across the street.

The Cordelia Benson Sanctuary, the sign read, as it had then. Below it was a new tagline: *Programs for Life.*

For a moment, Anne couldn't breathe, couldn't speak past the tangled sorrow and fear and dread sitting like a boulder on her diaphragm. Some of the best—and worst—moments of her life had happened behind that genteel, tasteful facade.

She closed her eyes and focused on her breathing, a technique that was supposed to help disperse tension. It didn't make a dent now. Abandoning that attempt, she forced herself to speak. "Davis, there's something else I never . . . I never told you." Through the tightness in her chest, she managed to suck in enough air to continue.

"I gave birth to a child." She pointed, her finger shaking. "In that house. When I was seventeen years old."

Grace

"What's that you're making?" Grace asked, slipping her arms into a cardigan. After yesterday's wonderful weather, today had dawned gray and chilly.

Charlotte held up the glass to study the contents, a spoonful of yogurt in the other hand. "Strawberry, blueberry, and yogurt parfaits, with granola."

"They look yummy." Grace wandered over to the coffeepot and poured a mug. An aroma of sizzling sage floated her way. "You're serving that new local sausage, I take it?"

"Yes. And scrambled eggs." Charlotte set the glass down then plopped the yogurt on top. "I was thinking of a cold breakfast but it's so damp. They'll need something hot."

"I'll light the gas fire in the dining room," Grace said. "That will take the chill off."

Charlotte placed the parfait glasses on a tray. "I'm right behind you."

In the dining room, Grace turned on the fireplace while Charlotte arranged the glasses on the sideboard. "Are we still on for shopping?" Charlotte asked.

Grace held her hands out to the warmth already radiating from the flames. "Absolutely. It's actually a good day to go shopping. If it was nice out, I'd be thinking about all my garden chores."

Charlotte snorted. "The gardens look fantastic. Better than ever." She pivoted to face the French doors. "I can't say the same for him."

Outside the glass stood a man with a large flat tan hat with white cotton fluff on top. In the middle he wore baggy red-and-white spotted clothing, and his legs were also clad in tan.

Grace put a hand to her head with a groan. "Someone else who didn't get the memo?"

"What's he supposed to be?" Charlotte's brow cleared. "Oh, a strawberry shortcake, I bet."

"Not too appetizing," Grace muttered as she crossed the carpet. "Good morning," she said when she opened the door. "Why don't you come in?" Rain was starting to patter down and she didn't have the heart to leave him out there.

The man sidled through the door, his puffy clothing almost too wide for the opening. "Thanks. I hoped I'd make it before it started pouring." As if listening, the rain began to sheet down with a hissing roar, obscuring their view of the garden.

"How'd you get here?" Charlotte asked.

"I rode my bike," the man said, straightening his headpiece. "The wind was a challenge. Almost lost my hat a few times."

Maybe that would have been a blessing. Grace bit back a smile. "Well, you're not going to like what I have to say. We're not a judging station. The ad was wrong."

Charlotte held out one of the parfaits. "But you can eat this, if you want. Before you call a cab."

By the time their visitor left, his bicycle sticking out of the cab's trunk, the two couples had come down to breakfast. Anne looked years younger, Grace noticed, as if a burden had lifted. She said a silent prayer of thanks while going around the table with the coffee carafe.

"This looks great," Davis said, picking up one of the parfaits.

Sean spooned up a hearty mouthful. "It's delicious. We should have these at home, hon."

Bridget winked at Grace. "I've been trying to get him to eat yogurt for years. You and your sister have the magic touch."

Grace set the empty carafe back on the burner and started a fresh pot. "I'm glad to hear that." She turned to Davis. "Is this weather going to ruin your golf plans?" The rain had lessened but was still coming down.

The older man shrugged. "Naw. I'll wear a slicker. Takes more than a little rain to stop me."

Sean gave a belly laugh. "That's what I'm talking about. Up north we play in the snow. With fluorescent orange balls of course."

"Why don't you come with me today?" Davis suggested. "The girls are going shopping."

Bridget's husband liked that idea and the two men began to swap golf stories.

"Look what you started, Grace," Bridget said with a mock eye roll. "They'll be obsessed with golf all day."

Anne nudged Bridget. "That's fine with me. After we go shopping, I want a mani-pedi." She held out her hands and studied her nails. "This manicure bit the dust at the beach."

Bridget made a similar gesture. "I don't even have nail polish on right now. Getting a manicure would be fun."

Charlotte ferried out platters of eggs, sausage, and toast. Grace helped her place the offerings on the table.

Sean put his empty parfait glass aside. "The yogurt was good but I'm so glad there's more."

"Me too." Davis wiped his mouth with his napkin and sighed. "We'll need lots of energy to make eighteen holes."

Curt came striding into the dining room. He smiled a greeting then slid into a chair at the end of the table, next to Bridget. "Just in time, I see," he said, nodding at the platters.

Grace brought him a mug of coffee. "Good morning, Curt.

What are you up to today?"

"Not sure." Curt said thanks, then poured cream into the mug and stirred. He studied the wet garden. "Presley's working, so . . ."

"You play golf?" Davis asked. "We're going." He motioned between himself and Sean. "We'll find a fourth at the club, no sweat."

Curt cocked a brow. "Don't all doctors play golf? That'd be nice, thanks." He took a tentative sip of the hot brew. While the platters went around under Grace's watchful eye, Curt leaned toward Bridget. "Presley and I are back on track," he said in a low voice. "Whatever you said to her yesterday worked."

Bridget helped herself to scrambled eggs. "I'm glad to hear that. Though it wasn't anything special."

Grace couldn't hold back a smile. She'd been rooting for the young couple ever since the scene in the garden. She picked up the empty toast platter. "Anyone want more toast? I'll go make some."

After breakfast, the men left for the course and, a short while later, the women were ready to go downtown. Grace drove, since her Honda CR-V had plenty of room for passengers and purchases both. Despite the wet weather, visitors dressed in bright rain garb milled about the park and some of the festival booths were open. But the ladies' destination was Miss Millie's, on Main Street, so Grace steered toward downtown.

Cars lined the street but Grace found a spot near the dress emporium. They piled out and headed along the sidewalk. "Davis and I have been married over thirty years," Anne said, "and I still get a flutter about stepping out with that man."

"Me too, with Sean," Bridget said, walking in tandem with Anne. "Although it's only seventeen years for us."

"You're both so fortunate," Grace said, experiencing a pang. If only she and Hank . . . she thrust aside that train of thought. She'd been a widow a long time. She knew how to deal with the emotions by now. Usually.

Charlotte had been studying the shop windows as they walked along. She stopped and pointed at the display in Miss Millie's. "That's the dress I want."

Grace studied the dress, imagining Charlotte wearing it. The knee-length sky-blue frock was sleeveless, with silver embroidery on the bodice and a tulle overskirt. Frothy and feminine, but simple, as suited her sister's style. "It's perfect."

"I like that one," Bridget said in a soft voice. The dress she was pointing to was floral, with a handkerchief hem.

The pale rose, green, and cream print would set off Bridget's dark hair and eyes, Grace thought. "Also perfect," she said. A pulse of excitement made her shiver in delight. What was more fun than shopping for a pretty outfit? "Come on, let's go inside."

Miss Millie's had plenty of dressing rooms, so they could all try on things at the same time. The manager, Sophie Mah, was the perfect mix of attentive and hands-off. "Let me know if you need another size, ladies," she said as they were browsing the racks. "I'll grab it for you."

"Have things been good?" Grace asked, holding up a pale-green silk wrap dress with tiny ruffles at the neck. She knew Sophie from the chamber meetings.

"Surprisingly yes," Sophie said, straightening a pile of cotton sweaters with nimble fingers. "Even though the festival is a couple of blocks away, I've had lots of new customers."

"That is your dress," Charlotte said, stabbing a finger at the green silk. She held the one from the window. "Try it on."

"Yes, ma'am," Grace said with a laugh. She chose one more then carried the two dresses behind the curtain. The green dress slipped over her head and settled on her torso as if it'd been made for her. She adjusted the neckline and the sash. *Not bad*. Now she needed opinions from the others.

When she slipped out, the silk swishing around her legs, she saw that Bridget and Anne were already standing in front of the mirrors, wearing almost identical expressions of hope and doubt. They turned their heads in unison when Grace joined them.

"Wow, that dress looks gorgeous on you, Grace," Bridget said. She was wearing the floral, which fit her tall, curvy body perfectly.

"The color looks great with your hair and light tan," Anne added. The older woman was dressed in a pale-pink fit-and-flare dress that suited her petite frame.

Another curtain pushed aside with a dramatic jingle of the rings. "I told you it was the one, Grace." Charlotte sashayed across the carpet in bare feet, wearing the blue dress. She smoothed the overskirt and turned to and fro. "I like it."

Sophie clapped her hands. "Ladies, you are lovely. The gentlemen are going to fall in love."

Bridget and Anne giggled. "I hope so," Bridget said.

Grace was happy for her guests. A romantic dinner dance with their husbands was a perfect way to end their stay at Magnolia Harbor Inn. And it had been far too long since she, herself, had been dancing.

27

Anne

Anne opened the wardrobe door, then pulled her new dress out of the bag. As she placed it on a hanger, she noticed a couple of wrinkles, nothing too bad. It would be fine by tomorrow night, when she'd be wearing it.

She'd had a wonderful time with the other women. After leaving the boutique, they'd had lunch then poked around downtown, including Judith's shop, Spool & Thread, and The Book Cottage. She needed more of that in her life, positive female companionship. All of them were young enough—well in Grace's case, almost—to be her daughters. But they'd treated her like a peer, not like someone from an older generation.

Sunlight burst out of the clouds and Anne went to take a closer look at the view. Droplets of rain glistened on the veranda, the trees, and the grass, while a brisk wind rapidly cleared the sky. Good. Maybe she and Davis could go back to The Tidewater tonight and eat on the deck. Alone this time. The thought gave her a shiver of pleasure.

She was still in awe about the new state of her marriage. Davis had been wonderful, so caring, when she'd finally revealed her deepest secret. He hadn't rejected her or judged her at all. He'd even apologized for his blunt, thoughtless remark about adoption the other night when they were talking to Bridget. "This is where the humble comes in," he said. "Tell me about it," she replied, and they laughed together. And cried.

Anne looked through the novels she'd purchased, choosing one to read. Next she looked at the baby quilt kits she'd been unable to resist. She'd gotten one pink and one blue, figuring that she'd make both, in anticipation of a grandchild someday. She could always save or give away the other, depending on what Austin had. With her sewing speed, it wasn't any too soon to start.

The suite door opened, to reveal Davis. "Hey, there." His grin was wide. He shucked his damp windbreaker and carried it to the bathroom to dry. "Before you ask, I left my muddy shoes and golf clubs in the car."

"Did you have a good time?" she called. "I did."

"Oh, yeah," came the reply. "They're great guys." He bustled back into the room. "I had a thought, Anne, while I was on the course."

She packed the quilt projects in her suitcase. "What was that?" She picked up the three books she wasn't going to read and put those in there too. Good thing they were driving instead of flying. Her suitcase was definitely going to be heavy.

He moved closer, until he was standing right over her. "Anne, look at me." His face was serious, a contrast to his light mood a moment ago. "There's a website where you can post information about your daughter. You might be able to find her that way."

A rush of heat washed over Anne, making her fingers tingle and her chest tighten. *Find her daughter?* The child she'd given up for adoption? Was such a thing possible?

Could her daughter be looking for *her*?

Of course she'd wondered about just such a thing over the years, but every time the thoughts came up, she squelched them. Shoved them into a drawer and kept it closed. Locked up tight, like her deepest needs and emotions.

But now that the secrets were no longer secrets—at least from the man she loved—maybe, just maybe, it was time.

A cry burst from Anne's mouth, followed by tears, surprising her as much as Davis, who bent over, murmuring soothing words. Anne put her hands over her face, trying desperately to control her sobs. "Oh, Davis. Yes. Let's do it. Maybe"—her voice shook—"maybe we'll find my baby."

After the sobs stilled, another thought floated into her mind. *Forgive.*

The still, small voice she'd come to know and trust was talking to her. Maybe it was time for her to listen to it—really listen.

Forgive.

She looked into her husband's eyes and saw only love, the deep, abiding kind that made what she was about to do possible. "I need to make a stop before the dance. Will you come with me?"

28

Bridget

"Honey?" Sean rapped on the bedroom door. "Do you think Grace has an iron?"

Bridget shifted in the bathtub, startled from her soporific daze. She wiped honey-scented bubbles from her chin and called, "I'm sure she does. If you can find one, I'll do it." Sean, competent at almost everything, was hopeless with an iron.

"I'll go ask." His footsteps receded and a moment later she heard the suite door close.

Almost time to get ready, anyway. Tonight was the dinner dance at the pavilion in the park. Extra tents had been brought in for shelter, and the advance menu Bridget had seen was mouthwatering.

But she was rooting for Charlotte. All the guests were. The kitchen this afternoon was a scene of barely suppressed frenzy as the chef prepared for the contest.

Bridget lifted an arm out of the water then pressed a finger into her skin, revealing a slight sunburn. Earlier that day, she and Sean had driven down to the coast for a picnic, the bright sun soon tinting their winter-fair complexions. After only one day of rain, the good weather was back, just in time for the festival's capstone event.

A day in the fresh air and sunshine had helped her shake off the latest disappointment. Presley had texted her to report that no baby girls were born in Magnolia Harbor on Bridget's birthday, or even that week. The town had been tiny back then.

She had no idea where to go from here. None. Not a one.

Maybe there was nowhere to go from here.

She hoisted herself out of the tub and reached for a fluffy towel from the heated rack. Grace and Charlotte certainly knew how to do things right. But beyond that, they'd created a home away from home for their guests.

She'd miss them. Struck by this realization, Bridget paused in her drying. She and Sean would have to come back. With Molly, of course. She'd love it here.

Besides, Annabelle's story required more research, right? Lots and lots of research.

Heartened by that thought, Bridget finished toweling off, then paused to plug in hot curlers. Tonight she was going all out: curled hair, makeup, a gorgeous new dress.

"I've got it," Sean called from the bedroom. "And an ironing board." Squeaking sounds announced that he was setting up the latter.

Bridget put on a robe, also provided by the inn, and joined her husband. Davis had mentioned that a dress shirt and slacks were fine for Sean to wear the dance. In the south, men's attire was more casual than up north. Davis said hardly anyone wore a suit, ever, and ties were for weddings and funerals only.

After ironing Sean's shirt and giving his slacks a touch-up, Bridget wound her long hair on the hot curlers. "Want a glass of iced tea?" Sean asked. "We have time."

"Sure." Bridget swished back out to the main room and accepted a glass. Her phone buzzed with an incoming call. *Becky*. Who was that? After a second, she realized. The docent from the Jackson House Museum.

"Bridget," Becky said when she answered, her voice sounding breathless. "I finally spoke to the trustees about Olympia's family. One of them is going to be here later." She named the time. "Can you stop by?"

Bridget eyed the time. If they hurried to get ready, they could do it, before the dinner started. "We'll be there, Becky."

Was this an answer to her prayer or another dead end? As Bridget slipped her locket over her head, she realized she was about to find out.

29

Anne

Anne took Davis's arm. "This is it. My family home." Her husband's eyes were wide as she led him up the path to the front door. As she'd hoped, the museum was still open. She opened the door and ushered him inside.

"What a place," he said, gazing around the cool entrance hall with its high ceilings.

Anne stopped to catch her breath, not because the walk from the car had been arduous. No, now that she was here, she needed to collect her thoughts and still her heart. A great teacher had told her once that forgiveness was an act of will, not emotion. She needed to trust that once she obeyed, the peace she sought would come.

Anne hadn't come to any great realization that her mother deserved forgiveness. No, the way she had treated her daughter was still wrong. Forcing Anne to give up her baby was the gravest injustice of all. *But none of us* deserve *forgiveness . . . it's a gift.*

That truth echoed in her mind as she crossed the polished floor to stand under the portrait. She tipped her head back and studied her mother's face. *Oh, Mama. I still don't understand everything about you, why you did what you did. But I forgive you.* She hesitated. *And I love you.*

With that thought, a sob burst from Anne, startling in the silence. She loved her mother, oh yes, she did, even though she was gone. Why else would her criticism and rejection cut so deeply? Tears gushed from Anne's eyes, the sorrow of a child for her long-lost mother. She dimly felt Davis's arm around her, heard his hushed words of comfort.

"Is she all right?" someone whispered.

Anne opened blurry eyes to see Bridget O'Brien standing there, her hand to the necklace she wore. Bridget's eyes were wide, filled with concern. For a moment, she studied the young woman's face. "Are you wearing a locket?" Anne asked.

Bridget nodded and held it out to Anne.

Roaring sounded in Anne's ears and the room was shifting around like that time she'd been in a storm at sea. Her vision narrowed until all she could see was the silver heart Bridget was holding.

"Have you been wearing it this entire time? Under your clothes?" she asked, her voice hoarse. "Does it say *Lula*?"

"Yes, it does." Bridget obligingly turned it over to display the engraving. "Do you know something about it?"

"It's mine," Anne whispered.

30

Bridget

Bridget wasn't sure she'd heard correctly. Clutching the locket, she asked through stiff lips, "This is yours?" At Anne's nod, Bridget turned to Sean, hovering at her side. She heard the words as if from a distance, as if someone else was saying them. She felt stunned, like she'd been hit, hard, and couldn't think.

Sean's gaze went back and forth between the two women. "I believe it, now that I take a close look at you both." He put an arm around Bridget, "Let's go talk somewhere a little more private." Several more visitors had arrived, chattering.

"The morning room," Anne said. They allowed her to lead the way toward the back of the house, to a small, comfortable room with many windows.

The two couples settled in on sofas facing each other, an odd silence falling. Bridget couldn't stop staring at Anne's lovely face, at the tears glittering in her dark eyes. Why had she never noticed that Anne had brown eyes too? For days, they'd been staying at the inn, chatting, laughing, even shopping together, and she'd had no idea . . .

The enormity of this discovery, this sudden, unexpected answer to her prayers, was almost too much to take in. She clasped her hands together between her knees so tightly her knuckles went white. "Are you really my mother?" Bridget whispered.

"I am if you were born on—" Anne murmured the date. Bridget's birthday. She too appeared transfixed by this turn of events. "That's the date my baby was born." The tears welled, trickling down her cheeks. "I can't believe it. You're so beautiful." She turned to Davis. "Isn't my daughter *beautiful*, Davis?"

"She is, honey," he said, patting her hand. "Just like you."

The door opened, and they all turned at this interruption. "Bridget, there you are." Becky Thomas, the docent, bustled across the rug. "You just missed the trustee. But guess what?" She waved an envelope. "He left a letter for Olympia's daughter, in case she happens to turn up. When Julep told him about the necklace you were wearing, he wondered if this was meant for you. He said he always thought Olympia's daughter would come back."

Anne gave a grunt of laughter and stood, her cheeks still wet with tears. "I'm Tallulah Anne Jackson. That letter is for me."

Becky stared down at the envelope, then up at Anne, her mouth gaping. "That's the name all right. Wow, this is amazing."

"And I am her daughter," Bridget said, moving to stand beside Anne. At this admission, Bridget experienced a wave of powerful exhilaration that made her shake. By some miracle, she had found her mother, her safe harbor, at last.

Anne

Anne's feet barely touched the ground as the two couples walked across the waterfront park toward the dinner venue. She was still reeling from the latest turn of events. "Thank you," she whispered, staring up into the heavens at the glittering stars and tender moon. She had the feeling she'd be offering thanks for a long time to come. She stole yet another glance at Bridget and a thrill rushed through her. *Her baby.* No doubt she'd be experiencing that same burst of delight again and again too.

Canopies had been set up around the lawn, round tables covered with cloths placed in their shelter. Candles on each table flickered, revealing gorgeous floral centerpieces.

"There's Grace," Davis said, indicating a table where Grace sat with a man. That must be the neighbor she'd mentioned, Spencer Lewis. She'd promised to save a table for the inn guests. Davis guided her in that direction, with Bridget and Sean following.

Strings of tiny white lights enclosed the area, beyond which ticket holders were allowed. As they entered, Anne saw Nancy Blackstock Higgins trotting across the grass, moving fast for someone wearing stilettos. She practically screeched to a halt when she saw Anne and Davis.

A spiteful expression twisted Nancy's features. "There you are. I half expected you to hightail it out of here. Again."

Anne remembered something. Nancy had been in love with Beau. That must be the source of her malice and bitterness. "No, Nancy, afraid not." She pulled Davis closer. "My husband and I are having too nice a time visiting my old hometown."

Nancy whirled to face Davis. "Did she tell you about Beau? About the baby?"

Anne had thought she wasn't capable of being shocked any more that evening. But Nancy's words stole her breath. *Nancy knew?* Despite all of Olympia's efforts to keep the pregnancy secret, people in town had known.

Davis smiled. "She sure did. In fact, she's right there." He tipped his chin toward Bridget and Sean, who had gone ahead and sat down. "I'll introduce you, if you like."

Nancy stumbled backwards, both hands up. "That's okay," she muttered. She turned and trotted away, moving even faster than before.

Without comment, Davis escorted Anne to the table.

Grace greeted them, and then introduced them all to Spencer. "Feel free to go up and grab plates." She pointed. "Charlotte's up there somewhere, with the other chefs." They had a plate of vegetables and dip she'd been picking at, it looked like. "We're going up right now too."

"I can fix you a plate, if you want," Davis said, pulling out a chair for Anne. After thirty-five years, he knew what she liked and how much to bring her.

"I'll do the same," Sean said, following the older man's lead. "Give you two a chance to catch up."

Anne settled in the chair and pulled it a little closer. Meeting Grace's eyes, she realized the innkeeper didn't even know the big news.

Bridget spoke first, taking Anne's hand. "Grace? I want to introduce you to my mother." Her smile was tremulous with emotion. "Anne, I mean Tallulah Anne, is my birth mom." She gazed at Anne with affection. "We just found out tonight."

Grace looked from one to the other, speechless, then gave a squeal of delight and joy as she jumped up out of her chair. "That is incredible. I'm so, so happy for you." She hugged them both.

Spencer looked on, slightly confused but smiling. "Congratulations, ladies." He stood. "Shall we go up, Grace? Or I can get you something."

"No, I'll go." Grace fell into step with Spencer, sending Anne and Bridget another smile.

"I think she did that on purpose," Bridget said. "To give us a few minutes alone."

"Grace is wonderful." Anne feasted her eyes on Bridget. "You're so much like him. Beau. Your father. Why didn't I see it before?"

"The Boston accent?" Bridget joked. They shared a laugh, then Bridget said, "Tell me about my dad. Is he . . . alive?"

Oh, poor baby. She doesn't know. "I'm afraid not, honey. But he died a hero." Anne told her daughter about Beau, his brains and kindness and good looks. How they'd been teenage sweethearts and planned to get married, after Beau finished boot camp. "But he never made it." Her voice trembled as she relayed the story of the helicopter accident.

"That's awful," Bridget said, the words heartfelt.

Anne squeezed one of Bridget's hands. "It certainly is. That's why I was so happy when I learned I was going to have you. Until my mother found out." *My mother, whom I now forgive.*

"That's why you gave me away?" Bridget's voice was a whisper. She hunched her shoulders, as if against a blow.

"It is." Anne sighed. "The *only* reason. Things were different in those days. Single women didn't often keep their babies. I was pressured until I gave in, until I agreed to go to the home in Charleston. Mama stood over me while I signed the adoption papers." Her lips twisted in a wry expression. "For a long time, I couldn't forgive my mother for that." She thought of the letter in her handbag. "But I did, just tonight. And then I learned that she regretted her decision."

"That's what was in the letter?" Bridget guessed.

"Yes, that and more." Anne was elated that her mother had finally said, "I love you." Even though it was decades too late and Olympia was gone, Anne cherished the words. "You can read it, when we have more time." Anne was very aware that the men would be coming back shortly.

Quickly she said one more thing. "I never forgot you, you know. I thought it was hopeless, since the adoption was sealed. But a day never went by . . ." Tears burned again. Anne had done her best to bury the past, feeling she had no choice, but she'd always carried a secret prayer in her heart for her baby's well-being and happiness.

"I love you, Mom." Bridget's grin was bright, so bright, rivaling the sun. "I'm so very thankful that we have the rest of our lives together."

Anne gave Bridget a hug. "I love you too. And we're going to make the most of every minute, I promise."

32

Grace

In the middle of dinner, Missy Perkins, dressed in a startling but flattering emerald-green satin frock, stood up at the bandstand microphone. "Good evening, everyone. Welcome to our dinner dance, the final event of Strawberry Fest. Wasn't the event fabulous, everyone?" The crowd burst into applause and cheers, as Missy had no doubt hoped.

The chamber director proceeded to recap the evening's events, including the entrée contest. "Ballots are in the middle of your tables, folks. After you eat, mark your top three choices. Someone will be around to collect them. May the best chef win, though in Magnolia Harbor, all our chefs are winners."

"I don't know if I'd put it that way," Spencer said under cover of the audience clapping.

Grace laughed, then picked up a ballot to look at the entries. There were five choices, the name of the dish the only identifying notation. In addition to Charlotte's chicken and Dean's scallops, there were savory strawberry quiche, pork medallions in a sauce, and a vegetarian Asian stir-fry. Grace had taken a tiny nibble of all of them, to be fair, but she liked Charlotte's entry best. She was pretty sure she wasn't just playing favorites.

Spencer nudged her. "What did Charlotte make?" He hadn't been involved in the recipe development.

Grace pointed at the chicken on his plate. To her amusement, he took a bite, exclaiming, "My goodness, this chicken is incredible.

One of the best things I've ever eaten." He spoke loudly enough that people at tables nearby turned their heads.

Charlotte shook her head with a smile, her blonde locks swaying. "I wonder who made these delicious scallops?" Her glance at Dean was teasing. After all her angst over the contest, her sister seemed content to let the chips fall where they may.

They had finished eating and were filling out ballots when Anne came over to Grace. "We'd like to extend our stay a couple of days, if our room is available." She turned to smile at Bridget, who was telling Davis and Sean a story with many gestures. "Bridget and Sean want to stay also and have the kids come. Molly can miss a day or two of school to meet us, my son, Austin, and his girlfriend. We're hoping to have an impromptu family reunion."

Grace thought back to the reservation system, which had revealed a troubling lack of bookings for next week but was now looking up. "We can do that." She reached for the woman's hand. "I'm so happy for you."

Anne's eyes glowed. "Thank you. I'm almost beside myself, I'm so excited." She glanced at Bridget again. "We have a lot of years to make up for. But it's going to be great fun doing just that."

"It will be." Grace was thrilled that the inn had played a part in this happy ending. And judging by how close Curt and Presley were sitting, whispering to each other, it looked like another happy ending was in the making.

An outburst across the table caught their attention. Dean threw back his head and laughed, waving a piece of paper in the air. "You're voting for *me*, Charlotte? Why would you do that?"

Charlotte stared down at the tablecloth, her cheeks flaming. She snatched her vote back, but didn't change it. "Because I'm honest and your scallops were better than my dish." Then she squared her shoulders and lifted her chin. "But I do have some suggestions for you."

Grace chuckled as her sister launched into a very thorough and technical critique of Dean's scallops. To her further amusement, the chef listened, rubbing his chin with a thoughtful expression. Although when she looked closer, his eyes were sparkling.

The ballots were collected and tallied during dessert. When the big moment was upon them, Missy Perkins took the microphone again. "Ladies and gentlemen, we're ready to announce the winners of tonight's contest. In third place we have . . ." A pause, then she said, "Asian stir-fry by Why Thai." The audience clapped.

Grace's belly tightened. Charlotte and Dean were both looking toward the front, seeming to be cool and collected. She was more nervous than they were, it appeared.

"And in second place, we have Strawberry Barbecue Chicken, by Magnolia Harbor Inn."

Charlotte's chin dipped a bit but then she turned to Dean with a smile. "You still have a chance."

He held up his hands, fingers crossed, and made a comical face of desperate hope. Everyone at the table laughed.

Missy rattled her paper, building the suspense, then said, "First place goes to Strawberry-Infused Scallops from The Tidewater."

Charlotte clapped, then looked smug. "I knew I picked a winner."

"You're a good sport and I like that," Dean said. He leaned toward Charlotte, dropping his voice into a serious timbre. "There's always next year."

Charlotte matched his tone. "And you'd better watch out, mister. Revenge, like May strawberries, can be sweet."

Grace shared a smile with Spencer at their banter. She had a feeling more wonderful experiences were on the way, not only for the guests but for the innkeepers of Magnolia Harbor Inn too.